Vi Khi Nao is an unstoppa[...]
zanily transporting and deliri[...]
me gasping this many times [...]

— Danielle Dutz, auth[...]

Vi Khi Nao's *THE VEGAS DILEMMA* is a kaleidoscopic jaunt
through the lives of the outcasts and artists and lovers who reside in The
City of Sin. Nao's prose is as sharp and strange as a buried blade. *THE
VEGAS DILEMMA* answers the question I've been asking myself for
years: What would happen if Robert Walser time-traveled to modern day
Vegas? You won't regret reading these stories.

— Alex McElroy, author of *The Atmospherians*

The more I read Vi Khi Nao the more I come to feel she is one of
those writers with a tinged mind, like a Brautigan, an Inger Christensen.
But more I should say these stories find ethics in their mutating formal
design and I read these at a moment of exasperation with fiction, if it
cannot stoop to be subsumed by ethics in a crisis. To name the names.
Mark Zuckerberg. Kavanaugh. Spit, spit! And part of this ethic, also, is
this flexing of wormholes, maybe probed by color, by incendiary meta-
phor-- a sudden cottontail. Or how each piece here is shaped for (whim-
sical, grave) escape.

— Caren Beilin, author of *Revenge of the Scapegoat*

In conventional fiction, characters are amplified by what they consume,
the places that surround them. In *THE VEGAS DILEMMA*, a nov-
el-in-stories, objects and places become characters themselves—active
agents of a state that advertises the possibility of authentic human connection and abundance, but whose destructive drive to consume everything (and everyone) within it finally denies intimacy. People in this hy-
per-real Vegas objectify and are objectified in turn, becoming, in Nao's
words, "human mirror, human pillowcase, human chopstick, human
sweater, human bathrobe." These strange, compelling and hallucinatory
stories expose the dehumanizing and ultimately lonely racial, sexual and
class politics of contemporary America.

— Paisley Rekdal, author of *Appropriate: A Provocation*

With handfuls of Cheerios and memories of bibimbap, Nao's stories restlessly wander the nocturnal streets, like a Jeanne Moreau in Vegas, desiring and dreading connection and intimacy. Tender and gimlet eyed, with the faintest whiff of desiccated despair, the prose is polished to perfection. A piercing and haunting book.

— Jeffrey DeShell, author of *Masses and Motets*

THE VEGAS DILEMMA is a saucy dinner date you wouldn't take for spaghetti. Vi Khi Nao has finally tackled impossibility and solved it. The gaze of this collection is toward a pile of raw and intimate donuts of temporality.

— Ali Raz, author of *Human Tetris*

Each of Vi Khi Nao's stories drops you flatfooted into a new world, finding yourself in a universe at once recognizable and fantastical, poetic and political. Each story lends its hand to a larger whole, but stands alone as an artifact of a place that never quite existed. These stories should be read slowly—each one a puzzle I found myself delighted to solve.

— Adriana E. Ramírez, PEN/Fusion award winning author of *Dead Boys*

THE VEGAS DILEMMA reminds me of riding buses in Santa Fe, or my first morning off in NYC when I foolishly ordered a cup of coffee and started reading *War and Peace* at a crowded midtown diner with a line that curved into the street. It reminds me of sitting in public spaces, anxiously, expecting that I'd soon be asked to leave or warily aware of some stranger in the periphery or some stranger who sits too close to me, or the stranger who relentlessly abducts my regard and stuffs it in his luggage compartment, where so much pleasure is sought and so much pleasure sold, and skirting this are the Starbucks, the bus stops, the Panda Express, a very specific loneliness.

— Jessica Alexander, author of *Dear Enemy,*

The Vegas Dilemma

Requests for permission should be directed to 1111@1111press.com,
or mailed to 11:11 Press LLC, 4732 13th Ave S, Minneapolis, MN
55407.

Cover Art by Tiffany Lin

Paperback: 978-1-948687-42-3 (paperback)

Printed in the United States of America

FIRST AMERICAN EDITION

9 8 7 6 5 4 3 2 1

The Vegas Dilemma

Vi Khi Nao

Earlier versions of these following stories have appeared in the following journals/ publications:

"The Human Camouflage." was featured in *Tyrant Hotel*.

"If the Wind Does Not Serve, Take The Genius to Her Limits." was featured in *Western Humanities Review*.

"Symmetry of Provocation." was featured in *The White Review*.

"Pulverized Oat Wheels." was featured in *Notre Dame Review*.

"Lonely Not Like A Cloud." was featured in *McSweeneys*.

"Field Notes On Suicide Or The Inability To Commit Suicide Or It's Hard To Follow A Pomeranian Around." was featured in *Powerhouse*.

"Capable of Giving Her Leprosy." was featured in *The Account*.

"Tools For Extinction: Ashan." was featured in *Lolli Editions*.

"Diurnal, Nocturnal." was featured in *Black Mountain Radio*.

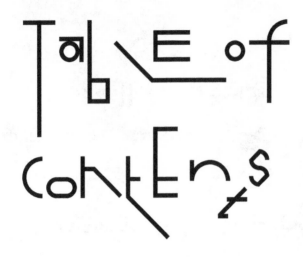

Table of Contents

PART I

Pulverized Oat Wheels / 17

Not Capable Of Giving Her Leprosy / 21

Mother Nature Is Belligerent / 25

Symmetry of Provocation / 33

Lonely Not like a Cloud / 40

If the Wind Does Not Serve, Take the Genius to Her Limits / 50

The Uzi Could Be a Landscape of Love / 57

The Human Camouflage / 63

Your Sadness Is Salt on Salt / 66

Field Notes on Suicide or the Inability to Commit Suicide or It's Hard
to Follow a Pomeranian Around / 68

PART 2

When the Memory Foam Mattress Refuses to Become the Next
President of the United States / 77

The Vegas Dilemma / 83

Football Bets Out of State / 88

May I Have Your Attention Please / 90

Callously Touched by This Maniacal Man / 92

In My Youth My Father is Short and Poor / 105

Ashan / 107

Diurnal, Nocturnal / 111

PART 3

The Man on the Bus Kept Finding Reasons to Touch Her / 121

The Woman with the Dense German Face Tries to Fall Asleep / 125

Calm, Calm, Calm, Rupture / 133

What I Starved before Turning You into Blue / 135

Vignettes: Exploration of Certainty & Uncertainty / 140

She Is No Longer on Vacation with a Hole / 145

The Fork Is Busy Spooning the Spaghetti / 151

Her Underwear, Pompeii / 155

Love Story with Bifurcation and Violation / 159

INTRODUCTION

Today is Wednesday, May 12th, 2021 and I'm in Claremont, California, writing a preface to Vi Khi Nao's collection of stories, *The Vegas Dilemma*. I've been tasked with this by circumstance, and I think it would best to begin by explaining. Slightly more than a year ago, I attended Vi's reading at Pitzer College, where she read poetry and prose, including from her collaborative book (with Ali Raz) *Human Tetris*, which consists of imaginary personal ads, written one per day. She also offered audiovisual evidence of her project of responding to filmmaker Leslie Thornton's *Sheep Machine*, which depicts sheep grazing in the Alps, by writing about each individual frame of the film. Vi's presentation had an uncanny quality of insouciance that was delightful. Rather than presenting her work the way a writer typically does, shoving it ahead of themselves like a cowcatcher on a locomotive, or wearing it protectively like a suit of armor, she appeared be standing alongside her work and encountering it with us.

Afterwards – and this is the more important part of this story – Vi and I went out with her host and a few other poets, to eat Italian food at a restaurant where through the whole dinner we for some reason had to sit on high stools. Vi surprised us by bringing out a flat box with a neat stack of her eloquent pen drawings contained inside. She told us they were for sale and I immediately picked out two for purchase. It was the first time I'd ever used Venmo on my phone. The day afterwards I took them to my office, intending to get them framed and hung. They ended up sitting in a folder on the desk where I placed them that day for over a year.

Vi and I both recall that night as "the last thing that happened before Covid." I just checked, and it was February 17th, 2020, a little earlier than I might have guessed. There might even have been another night in a restaurant after that, I don't recall. But there were no further readings, or gatherings after readings. There were certainly no new friendships forged instantly in person. Days later we all went into the year that needs little paraphrase, one of mourning and endurance but also, for those of us lucky enough, reflection. When a PDF of *The Vegas Dilemma* arrived recently, it felt inevitably like a kind of psychic bookend, or an unfreezing of a moment in time. And when Vi asked me to write something for it, I felt both honored and confused. What kind of preface did this work need? After we spoke on the telephone, however, I began to think of the invitation in a different light. Though this cycle of short stories takes a more traditional outward fictional form, Vi had enlisted me into a small piece of eleventh-hour gesture of collaboration. When we spoke, Vi confirmed what I felt, that the book had retroactively turned into an investigation into a universe about to suffer an enigmatic lull in its frantic activities. While the stories themselves were in no position to directly trace this synchronicity, and how it was echoed in our acquaintance, I was.

So that this preface isn't strictly self-referential, I'll say one or two more things about *The Vegas Dilemma*. Vi Khi Nao's fictional language is full of magical slippages, which remind me of Jane Bowles, Lydia Davis and Richard Brautigan. As with those writers, an esoteric sadness seeps up through surface deadpan and pizzazz. The stories are self-contained, but also form a cumulative meaning, even if it would be difficult to name directly. The ostensible glamor of Las Vegas reveals an undertow (I accidentally typed "undertown") of melancholy, which doesn't resolve, but extends. The word "thighs" seems to be a protagonist in a kind of proto-novel. I want to end by quoting Vi, not from our conversation, but from a wonderful interview in Bomb magazine: "When I produce a work, I don't view it as transformative. I see it more as an extension—an extension cord. You plug it into the wall, and it can get you only so far, and then you find another cord and add it to it, and you can listen to music a few miles down the road instead of where the outlet is."

Jonathan Lethem

PART 1

PULVERIZED OAT WHEELS

She had been kicked out of all venues, including the ones she spent money in.

At Smith's, they asked her not to use the tables and chairs. It was dark; around 11 pm. They had shut down the place for dining. When she sat down to eat the food she had bought at their grocery store, they told her that she couldn't. She packed all of her purchased food into her backpack and left.

She reasoned: a clerk, feeling threatened by her reticence and her ambitious aloofness, had complained to the manager that a patron was eating in the dark in the corner. He didn't understand her antisocial, pedestrian behavior. Her solitary presence made his eyes itchy. He wanted to get the Best Employee Award. His complaint led the manager to do something about it.

She stands outside eating her Cheerios by the handful. A few fall out of her hands and roll like diminutive beige wheels. When she walks forward, she crushes some and they pulverize immediately into oat dust.

She feels crushed by the Smith's employees' ignorance and lack of kindness, but she complies with their new regulations. She doesn't throw a fit and she doesn't fight them. She no longer sits at the table and chair at Smith's anymore. She doesn't understand why she shops at Smith's so often when they treat her so poorly. She thinks, "Sometimes we walk blindly through life because the closest grocery store is too close and the kindest grocery store is too far. We see distance as an inconvenience, but we don't see that what is near can make us nearsighted and our reliance on this nearness can handicap us. Our laziness isn't a monster, but something has to be. Monstrosity isn't labor intensive. Placing a gilded spoon into someone's mouth isn't the best way of making the nightshade family shady."

The least tactful member of the nightshade family isn't the eggplant, but the potatoes. The potatoes are always protesting, creating new labor laws, and behaving like Donald Trump. But the eggplant is cautious. Because they have the ability to soak a lot of olive oil, eggplants have to be careful whom they make fattest. Ireland, several times, had to go to war with potatoes. One day the potatoes relented.

Eggplants are more tactful because they are Lebanese. Middle-eastern cuisine forces them to be Arab-friendly. Eggplants make excellent friends and neighbors and possibly lovers.

She stands in front of the pub. The door doesn't click open as on most nights. As she walks away, the door un-clicks, but by then it is too late. She has decided that she will sit outside the pub to write.

The wind is small and tolerable, not large like several days ago.

She continues to chew her Cheerios by the handful. She understands why the pub doesn't want her. She doesn't gamble. She sits by the tall table in her high chair and drinks a glass of water without any ice and she orders different dishes from the menu, but rarely the same dish twice. She isn't combative and her energy is low. The pub wants her to stay at home and eat carrots.

Meanwhile, she sits outside on the bench a few steps away from the main door with the buzzer. Outside a large red neon sign lights up the words "Lounge Open 24 Hrs." The architecture gives off the impression that this could be a place where sex is sold for cheap. The buzzer protects the prostitutes. The buzzer has the ability to discern who is attractive and who is not. The buzzer is the key player here.

Soon she will go home to get ready for the airport. It's only midnight.

The last Uber driver who provided her service shared the same former profession as her father. He was a meat cutter on an assembly line for a meat processing plant. When his hands wouldn't let him slaughter cows anymore, the company forced him to embrace disability. Retired and handicapped and not amputated, he didn't know how to spend his time. His son suggested that he pursue Uber driving.

When the ex-meat-processing driver dropped her off, he told her that he would give her five stars. He told her, "I am going to give you five stars because you know I'm talkative and you conversed with me. I really appreciate that."

The man must be lonely, she thought. He was grateful that she spoke to him. Perhaps making money wasn't important to this man. Not being socially amputated from another human being was his primary vocation.

NOT CAPABLE OF GIVING HER LEPROSY

The streets seem young to her.

Vegas was built overnight with poor plumbing.

She is wandering the streets again.

Over orange chicken at Panda Express, he tells her that the white professor needs to return to the United States. He is white and he is having sex with his Korean students. He has been in Korea for about 1/5th of his life. His white dick hasn't touched the vaginal sewage system of North America for about a decade now. And, although modern Western plumbing doesn't miss him, apple pies donate a large part of their de-tarted, but not re-tarted, pastry life to craving him. His grandmother's nickname is PP (for Peach Pie) and his aunt's name is Rhubarb. He works for Bulgogi University, one of the best universities in Korea. It's where a female-dominated, English-curriculum-based education teaches female students how to learn English from sick, perverted, white faculty. It's not an expensive education. But there is no psycho-therapy there.

Professor Strawberry asks his young Korean student if she would have sex with him.

She says, "No." The bold young Korean student doesn't like strawberries in big batches. She prefers persimmons in boxes as gifts.

Professor Strawberry doesn't want to leave Bulgogi. At Bulgogi he has vocational and sexual power and prowess. Here, he has a grip on the upper echelon of South Korea's English literacy world. He is important. He is known. Certain female Korean students want to have sex with him. If he returns to the United States, he will need to develop a new hobby of internet porn, the pedophiliac kind—not related to lilacs—and may have to attend the same school, perhaps downgraded, as Harvey Weinstein and Kevin Spacey.

He leans over to tell her that although he has power, it's sort of fake. Like Professor Strawberry is technically powerful, but his power is borrowed or lent to him because he has blue eyes and white skin. True power is raceless or faceless, she discovers. Or color-deaf. In her mind, she doesn't think any of this is true. True power requires one to be dick-deaf. Is she dick-deaf? she asks her-self while she tries to stuff broccoli and beef into her mouth. She isn't hungry, but she is eating because it is easier to listen when one's mouth is full.

Meanwhile, about 6,000 miles away, in Las Vegas, eight Korean women in their late fifties huddle together in a Starbucks franchise to discuss the importance of eating meat while reading Han Kang's *The Vegetarian*. One woman turns to another woman, asking if it would be okay if she brought japchae to their next book club meeting.

"Ribeye fillet goes so well with glass noodle!"
"Of course!"
"Yes, of course!"

Literature is predominately a female vocation in Korea. Writing would make men effeminate, and Korean culture, like all other cultures, thrives on masculinity or bibimbap.

They walk to Ben and Jerry's. After working at a law office accomplishing nothing, or so he tells her, he wants to treat himself to something sweet. She doesn't want ice cream but she gives in. The last time, she watched him lick his ice cream and it was like watching a white man giving a blowjob to another white man, and although blowing isn't her thing, climate change, especially on the tongue, is her thing. She has a thing for licking things over. She reconsiders his offer to buy her ice cream. Maybe through the ice cream, he is offering her a free blowjob. Anyone would take it up, right? Thinking things over is her thing.

Her father's girlfriend is bisexual.

Her bisexuality consists of two grapefruits and one rainbow trout. Frying fish is her thing. She likes her relationship with oil to be around 350 to 375 degrees.

She walks into Trader Joe's. It's a Saturday. It's crowded. Walking there led her to 7,342 steps. Everyone looks like they are wearing diapers and holding each other's hands and saying hello and kissing goodbye while waving their gluten-free potato chips at each other. Whenever they fart, the cushions on their diapers absorb the sound and smell and thus everyone at Trader's Joe is happy with each other. Diapers make everyone socially safe. When she exited Smith's just an hour ago, no adults were wearing diapers and they didn't even know who they were shopping with, let alone waving expensive organic cocoa at another. Whenever a shopper farts at Smith's, everyone knows who it is and if their last meal was at McDonald's or Jack in the Box. But at Trader Joe's, all pollution or inadvertent acts of social transgression are family-accepted and family-owned.

Before falling asleep, she tells herself: although she can't commit suicide now, her biggest revenge on God is the ability to do it later, when she can. When she is permitted to.

When the barks of tall palm trees fall on the streets of Vegas by the heavy zephyr or breaths of tumbleweeds, they look like the backs of armadillos. When she saw the barks for the very first time, walking to Walmart late one night, they startled her. She thought the wind was so strong that even the hard shells of the nine-banded nocturnal omnivorous mammals were not impervious to the brutal desert wind. But, upon closer inspection, she discovered that the bony plates of these evergreens were not capable of giving her leprosy. Walking to Walmart has a greater chance of giving her nerve damage.

MOTHER NATURE IS BELLIGERENT

She wonders if she would sleep with him if she found herself desperate for money.

He has been watching her at the Starbucks inside of Smith's.

She knows, based on the way he keeps turning his shoulders and neck, that he wants her. Wants to do things to her that can only be found on the most popular porn websites. He pretends to wait for his Venti Iced White Chocolate Mocha, throwing furtive glances at her.

She doesn't invite his gaze and turns her shoulder away from him while she eats her fried chicken breast. When she notices that the chicken meat isn't white, she knows it has not been bleached or hasn't gone through epidermal hypnotherapy, the kind that transplants or replaces darker skin with white skin. She smiles because she hasn't seen *Get Out* and the chicken hasn't been asked to be racist or demonic.

She would give up Christianity in the blink of an eye. This is her silent response to reading the news about the Dapchi abductions on her phone while she evades the erotic gaze from the white man hovering above her. Boko has released around 100 girls, perhaps keeping one Christian girl who refused to refute her Christianity. Although she doesn't believe that Christianity is worth dying over, she doesn't think being Muslim is worth dying over either. So should she admit that religion is interchangeable? If religion has the ability to assume the role of a makeshift birth control, shouldn't she use it? If admitting that she is a Muslim even though she isn't prevents her from being raped by the Boko men—would it be like bringing a spiritual hatchet with you to a forest designed to induce sexual violence? She isn't a lesbian, but she does find it redundant: having one wife is already too much, but seventy? All those celestial mouths to feed in paradise. Even if they don't eat human food, they would need ecclesiastical food. Feeding is feeding. And, feeding more than zero requires work.

She isn't Muslim, but she likes the word "Mohammed."

Walking across the street at a very busy intersection, Horizon Ridge and Eastern, the light afternoon wind jogs her memory of last night's walk home. She had walked home from the pub at 3 am. The wind was uncontrollable and tempestuous. She remembers being angry at Mother Nature for being mean to her. She knows it was impersonal, but still she took it very personally. The wind was relentless and it kept spitting powerful forces of air at her. It forced her to walk backward, the wind with its thousand atmospheric hands pushing against her back. She felt like she was fighting with a mattress, a giant spineless fabric case filled with memory foam leaning its entire weight on her, forcing her to push back or be toppled. She took Mother Nature's transgression very personally. She remembers telling the wind that it was mean, but Mother Nature shrugged her shoulders. As if human moral systems were a fossilized, archaic, anachronistic nuisance. A defunct extinction. She wanted to punch the face of the wind, but she knew it would be useless.

Crossing the street, she takes a handful of Cheerios and stuffs them into her mouth. She has developed a positive proclivity for eating and walking. Something about vertical mobility (walking) on vertical mobility (eating) invites her libido to be generous with itself. She finds herself desiring sex while she ambulates from one traffic light to the next. But as soon as she stops walking and eating, her libido vanishes the way the wind itself vaporizes as soon as she enters Starbucks.

Before leaving the pub at 3 am, she had some strange encounters with the regular patrons, mainly gamblers. One patron kept punching his hands into the thin, slightly smokey air of the high-ceilinged pub. He behaved more like a professional basketball player than a gambler. Each time his gaming computer lit up with fake money sounds, he shouted with his mouth and hands. He celebrated his winnings kinetically: shouting and punching, and since there were only three patrons in the entire pub, his war cries stabbed the air with a sharpness that was closer to a hyena being raped by a lion than a white, muscular man who looked like a diminished Arnold Schwarzenegger. The violence of his winning was compelling. It broke one of the machines. The male server came around to his station, unlatched the computer's head, and revealed an intricate intestinal mess made of colorful wires, cords, power lines, and filaments. The server informed the gambling patron that a mechanic would be there in half an hour. The gambler retorted, "In seven to 24 hours, you mean?"

The server responded to his cynicism, "Yes, half an hour to seven hours."

The gambler had earned over one grand within five minutes of massaging the machine with his magical fingers. His lover, a woman, her luck was significantly different than his. She had been losing money. He leaned over her shoulder, trying to tell her how to make the move on her own screen. His win after win baffled her. The interior lining of her leather jacket was silk and leopard-printed, sprawled out on the high stool dressed in red leather. It looked fake. The woman was not fake. Her face expressed genuine torture, the torture of being around male success, and that energy spiraled her into a deep hopelessness. One day she would stun America the way head-shaved, bisexual, Cuban Emma Gonzalez stuns the world with her silence. Her anti-patriarchy rebellion would manifest itself most viscerally. And it would last 6 minutes and 20 seconds. Her white lover's success lasted more than 7 minutes. Until meeting him, she has been on the losing side of life for forty-something years.

By the time she climbs into bed, she is tired but wide-awake. Her pubic hair itches. She reaches down between many layers of fabric to scratch it. When she smells her hand, it smells like orange chicken and gardenia. She knows nothing about gardenia, but she once read an article online about how to kill it. In particular, she recalls the article's opening lines, "No one wants to kill a gardenia. Their creamy-white blossoms, so richly perfumed, are garden favorites, especially in the South."

Down south, where her pubic gardenia resides, the condition
of her garden isn't belligerent. Just acid-loving. Her pubic hair's
best friend is aluminum sulfate and doesn't need a humidifier.
The most female version of herself needs a body suit, the one
future cop Kiera Cameron wore in the Canadian sci-fi TV series
Continuum. A body suit that could self-heal, is continuous and
holographic, and has a polymeric nano-composite body carapace
with integrated, electromagnetic offensive and defensive capa-
bilities. Made of copper, the CPS suit has a memory system that
documents telemetry, and when she last touched herself.

What is the most female version of herself?

Would the most female version of herself sleep with the Starbucks guy?

When the mind is desperate, the body is most willing. Her
fingernails are so long now. Long fingernails are a symbol of her
lack of sex drive.

Her libido is a finger that grows one long nail, and God invents
Facebook to teach us about informational pornography.

When she walks home that night, the armadilloic evergreens
are trying to boycott leprosy from casinos and the strong winds
ambush them in many thorny bushes. When Moses emerges
from the thorn, God is trying to tell Facebook that prophet
Aaron, Moses's brother, shouldn't be forgotten for his diploma-
cy and his compromising and compassionate methods. And if
Facebook doesn't publicize this important attribute of Aaron on
permanent digital grounds, he will give Facebook a digital flood
that will wipe out all biblical and nonbiblical data. Instead of giv-

ing Zuckerberg the rightful bid to build a digital ark, he would anoint Elon Musk in his place.

Elon Musk has been trying to tell God that he is busy attempting to get humans to Mars.

GOD: Leave Mars to me, and delete yourself off Facebook.

ELON MUSK: What about Instagram?

GOD: Well, we'll see.

ELON MUSK: Instagram is a sibling of Facebook, like Aaron is to Moses.

GOD: Everyone likes Aaron more than Moses.

ELON MUSK: That's because he is so much more eloquent. Are you suggesting that we keep Instagram?

GOD: When that child floated down the Nile in that basket, I didn't think the Egyptian princess would love him so much.

ELON MUSK: She didn't love him that much.

GOD: She drew him out of the water and saved his life, which equates to great love.

ELON MUSK: When she made that announcement, biblical historians thought she had made a grammatical mistake.

GOD: The princess didn't make a grammar error.

ELON MUSK: Are you saying that her words were prophetic?

GOD: That's right, Elon! She drew him out of the water of the Nile and he helped me draw the Israelites from the Red Sea.

ELON MUSK: Language is a river of useful information and events.

GOD: And, my God, how Mark bastardized it.

ELON MUSK: Mark, one of the authors of the bible? Your Son's playmate?

GOD: Mark Zuckerberg.

ELON MUSK: Ah, that Mark.

GOD: Elon, I know you want to die on Mars.

ELON MUSK: I sure do.

GOD: If you PayPal—

ELON MUSK: If I PayPal you some money, would you help me?

GOD: I don't have a PayPal account.

ELON MUSK: I no longer own it, but I'll set one up for you.

GOD: I don't know how I feel about Peter.

ELON MUSK: I know. I know. Peter betrayed your Son three times. You can't trust him, but he can be trusted.

GOD: I meant Peter Thiel.

ELON MUSK: We co-founded PayPal together, but that was a long time ago. You don't trust Peter or his recent amicable relationship with Bitcoin?

GOD: No. No. Not that. I meant, he was the first Goliathic investor of Facebook.

ELON MUSK: You are not a fan of Mark or anyone that may have supported him.

GOD: I just don't want him to replace me, you know.

ELON MUSK: My God, if you combine all of your Abraham- ic customers, you have, give or take, two or three billions more customers than Mark's.

GOD: But, still, I worry....

ELON MUSK: Fear not.

GOD: I don't need a PayPal account. I am happy to know about your successful rocket launch.

ELON MUSK: That falcon is a beauty.

GOD: Indeed.

ELON MUSK: I don't even know who Mark is, but I'll be happy to be anti-Mark for humanity. I'll try to be the guardian that my father was not.

GOD: Your stepsister.

ELON MUSK: My stepsister, most unfortunate. My nephew is my father's son.

GOD: You said it was my plan. Not mine.

ELON MUSK: I know.

GOD: Telling your father that he is evil is not a deterrent.

ELON MUSK: What is then?

GOD: I don't know.

ELON MUSK: But you are God.

GOD: Yes, it is because I am God that I don't know. If I were not God, I would know.

SYMMETRY OF PROVOCATION

She saw her father at Smith's. By accident. She was paying the heat bill. After paying the heat bill, she deposited some of the money he had given her for rent. As she walked out of Aisle 6 near the cereal, she saw him. His eyes were looking up, searching for something. But she saw him. She decided that when he turned his gaze towards Captain Crunch he couldn't possibly see her. Walking past him quietly, she snuck out of his view. Her father was wearing a black sweater and black jogging pants. He looked scrawny and not like her father. Whenever she saw her father, her heart ached. Especially from a distance, from a place where he couldn't reciprocate her gaze.

Her father had suffered extensively during his sixty years of existence. Since arriving in the States in his thirties, he had worked for the poultry factory for nearly thirty years, and when he retired he was penniless, not from gambling, but from poor money management. After all, her father never had a high school education. He dropped out of school when he was 15 to join the

Army, fighting against the communists and Viet Cong. When the war ended, no one wanted to hire him, especially those from the North, moving South after the evasion. He was a white sheet of paper that no one wanted. So her father worked for a truck company that transported fruits and vegetables from the highlands of Vietnam into the cities. He transported goods from Ha Giang, Lao Cai, Quang Ninh, and even from Dalat. He transported Japanese plums, Asian pears, etc. Domestic market was his expertise.

For three weeks now, she hadn't spoken to him. Despite sharing the same bedroom and same bed, she hadn't technically spoken to him. She had purposefully been avoiding him. She hid under the bedsheets in the late morning, concealing her face beneath a mask of fabric. Sometimes the fabric clung to her nose and for moments she felt suffocated as if a cat had been sitting on her face and inhaling all her human breath. She had been concealing her face from him because she has gotten fat from eating too much cereal and pomelo. She had been eating too many fruits. When others asked her if her father worked for the university, she said that he worked in poultry. But they had a way of mishearing her.

'So he worked in poetry. What's that like?'
'They spend a lot of time decapitating heads and cutting thighs off sestinas,' she wanted to retort. But she said nothing. It was not her duty.

Her father's fingers didn't work properly most of the time. He experienced phantom pain and his severe carpal tunnel syndrome sometimes made it hard for him to hold a knife to cut a papaya. Papayas, by nature, are soft and delicate and require little strength to incise, but her father struggled at the kitchen counter. Sometimes she grabbed the fruit and knife from him and began to attack it gently.

She thought that after working on an assembly line, slaughtering 140 chickens per minute with his co-workers, he would have grown tired of eating chicken, but chicken was her father's favourite meat. It was a white meat that was easy for his body to digest. He didn't enjoy beef very much because his weak teeth found it hard to chew, and pork had a bloody smell that made him think of the North and of his sister who had breastfed him. His mother gave birth to thirteen children. He was the youngest and when her nipples grew pruney, his sister took over the breast-feeding. Sucking on his sister's teats was not meant to be a part of his life's journey but when he came out into the world as the thirteenth child, it had to be. His family couldn't afford formula.

'I don't want you to fry fish in the kitchen. Take it outside,' he told her a month ago, when she was still speaking to him. 'I don't want my girlfriend to leave me because we smell too fishy.'

'She doesn't care,' she told him.
'I don't want her to tell me that whenever she visits our place, she is visiting a fish market.'
'She won't leave you because of the smell.'
'If we emit less odour, our lovers stay with us for longer.'
'What about Napoleon?'
'What about him?'
'He didn't want Josephine to bathe for days before his arrival.'
'Smelling fishy and being acidic are two different things. Maybe Napoleon didn't eat enough navel oranges when he fought in battles and needed it from her when he returned home.'

'What is the point of having love if you can't be yourself with that person?'

'Smell you can change, but not personalities.'

'Does she love you, Dad?'

'She loves me a lot.'

'How does she show it?'

'I told her that her regular visits with the Botox doctor hurt my feelings and she stopped going.'

'Really? It hurt your feelings?'

'Well, yeah. After her Botox visits, her face always looked like the flappy, slimy insides of chicken wings. I told her that I've had to deal with that for thirty years and don't know if I can take another thirty.'

'She stopped going just like that?'

'Yeah.'

'What else?'

'I told her that I love phở gà and ox tail soup very much and so for the past six weeks, we have been to Viet Noodle Bar, Plumeria, and District One. We stopped eating so much of what she liked.'

'What does she like to eat?'

'Italian food like pappardelle.'

'She stopped?'

'Yeah. I told her Italian food makes her fat and Viet food doesn't.'

'I don't think it's wise to tell a girl that she's fat.'

'She lost 10 pounds since being with me.'

'Is she happy with that?'

'I don't know. She is really open about talking. She says, "Don't wait to tell me what's wrong with our relationship. Tell it to me now and we deal with it."'

'So you tell her what's wrong with her and not the relationship.'

'Well, she doesn't think acceptance makes a long-lasting rela-

tionship. Communication does. There are certain things I can't accept about her. It's just not fair.'
'What are they?'
'She eats so fast.'
'Is it her fault?'
'She can't help who she has become.'
'From eating too fast?'
'Yes.'

Her father's girlfriend was bisexual. Her father feared that she would be interested in his daughter, so now they avoided spending time with her. When his girlfriend gave his daughter a red dress, her father thought she was hitting on his daughter. He grew jealous and afraid of losing her. When his girlfriend invited them to dine together at The Black Sheep, run by Vietnamese executive chef Jamie Tran, her father became livid. He thought that his girlfriend wanted to court his daughter too. Meanwhile, his daughter sat alone in the kitchen, eating non-fishy meals and fighting back tears. Outside of her father's social circle, she had no social life. Her father's friends and lovers were her friends. She didn't know how to make her own friends.

So when she saw her father at Smith's, she pretended that it wasn't him. She felt his low self-esteem under the low, bright light of Smith's. During their long marriage before the divorce, her mother would remind him that he was a useless, penniless, namby-pamby man. Each time he tried to be intimate with her, she could hear through the thin wall of their adjacent bedrooms her mother asking him, 'Are you useless?'

He would reply candidly, 'I am useless.'
'What is the size of your penis, useless man?' she asked him.

'Very small.'
'What kind of a man did I marry?'
'A coward.'
'And what else?'
'A useless coward.'
'What else?'
'A useless coward with a tiny penis.'
'See how fast you're learning?'

His daughter wasn't the type to see a glass as half-full or half-empty. She had a practical way of viewing the world.

When she sat alone eating by herself for weeks and months, her father not allowing her to join in his dining experiences with his girlfriend, she thought, 'Does my father ever pity me or even love me?' She didn't want him to feel guilty for his happiness, but could he be truly happy if she wasn't?

As time passed, it dawned on her that her father was capable of enjoying happiness without her. In fact, he enjoyed his happiness more when she wasn't a part of it.

Meanwhile the father thought: his girlfriend was amazing at giving fellatio. He'd had to force his ex-wife to do it, but his girlfriend begged for it. So tossing his daughter aside was something he had to do. His happiness over her happiness. Life made him choose. So he chose. But could his daughter blame him? He had slaughtered so many chickens for his family. For thirty years, all he knew was chickens. It wasn't selfish now, was it, his wanting something for himself? If his girlfriend were to involve his daughter in their plans, he got the feeling that she would get into his daughter too. His daughter wasn't pretty but she was endowed with charisma. And charisma is a superior asset than beauty. Beauty ages, but charisma is timeless. Beauty is subjective, but charisma is universal. Beauty is temporary, but charisma lives on. He feared that his girlfriend would choose charisma over him. He wasn't a handsome man, but he had a smile and a warmness that drew others to him. It was the primary reason why his girlfriend learned how to say 'I love you' in Vietnamese.

It would be five more months before the lunar moon showed her face. What would he do between now and then, when his daughter had slowly become engorged like an overripe persimmon? He had come into the world to slaughter chickens for thirty years, to fight the Viet Cong for five years, to be a lame, penniless Việt Kiều, and to date this white woman whose teats were bigger than two pomelos.

And his daughter was a fish sitting on a cutting board, waiting for salt to be rubbed onto her. Her fins were long and whiskery. He held the cleaver tightly in his right hand. He and his girlfriend must have known that her head tasted the most delicious. They must have known. Why else would they lay her on the cutting board?

LONELY NOT LIKE A CLOUD

She recently returned to Vegas from a conference in Texas, where Joel Osteen recently denied humans affected by the flood shelter at his luxurious megachurch. Joel Osteen lectures and speaks sweetly, but his arms are the size of half-broken twigs. What would Jesus do?

Upon her return, another fellow Christian asks her if she will walk from Lake Mead to Hoover Dam with him and she says she would love to.

Since she is carless, he comes to collect her to take her to Lake Mead. They walk the long walk. She wears a long gray coat the color of postindustrial revolution, and blue jeans and a blue sweater and blue shirt to match the expansiveness of the sky. They walk the railroad passageway. Many other tourists, mostly fit, are walking along with them that day. They walk through the tunnels, tall and wide enough to fit the train's waistband. The tunnels have been carved or bombed or dug from mountainous rocks and there are short passages of open air with no mountains between them.

"How many days do you think it took them to carve through that large mountain?" she asks him.

"I think they blew through it with dynamite."

"Look here. They must have gotten excited by sanding the edges, but boredom and lack of time may have prevented them from finishing their sanding, because the rest seems very rugged."

"How many bombs do you think they went through to dig all of that tunnel?"

They walk somewhere. The wind passes through their coats and sweaters. She zips up her sweater and gathers the edges of her coat and hugs her own shoulders. It is only sixty degrees. When they are not under the vigilant gaze of the sun, it feels to her like forty degrees. No one else is wearing a coat. She looks like an Eskimoed bluebell among a sea of daffodils. But she doesn't seem to care and neither does he.

Eventually, they sit down on a sand-colored bench and look at the expansiveness of the blue lake before them. She takes out a grapefruit and a plastic container of precut mangos. She offers them to him and he takes the mango. Acidity does not get along with his stomach, but he takes one or two bites to show her that he is not a true asshole but a team player. He also eats the energy bar she offers him. He actually enjoys eating it and this diminishes her temporary guilt about his stomach's aversion to acidity. She wants to take the mango from him. She wants to take everything from him except his manhood.

A healthy woman with short hair, in shorts and in her late forties, runs past them.

"She is too healthy," she observes.

"Not your type?"

"She seems like a woman who is hard to be intimate with. I wouldn't want to date her."

"What do you mean?"

"If you were in the mood to have pancakes at 2 a.m., she wouldn't eat with you. She is too healthy. Intimacies are built around shared experiences. It's hard to get close to people who are rigid about their meals."

"Watching you eat those pancakes could be intimate too."

"Being as healthy as she is, she would prevent me from even preparing the batter, let alone placing the butter on the grill."

"Extremely healthy people are a danger to society."

They get up and they start walking again.

"Have I told you the story about what it is like to date a vegan?" he asked.

"No."

"She was obsessed about me not eating meat in front of her. She said, 'Are you going to eat meat in front of me? If you are, don't.' She wanted to control everything I did. That's not love. I don't think she loved me. We would do everything together. Have sex, watch movies, and do other things, but when it came to food, I couldn't eat what I wanted. And she was one of those poor vegans, too, so she couldn't afford to have expensive, healthy vegan meals. She would eat really bad vegan things, not beans and rice, but things without any moisture in them."

"Why does she need to eat food with moisture in it?"

"It keeps the food fresh."

"It does? I thought it was the opposite."

"She only ate vegan chips. She ate chips all the time."

"That's a lot of sugar and oil and starch."

"I know."

"I would try to leave her, but she would stalk me. She would find me and throw a smoothie at my windshield and try to get me to come back to her. I tried to come back but she returned to her old ways and wanted me to be vegan like her. Why couldn't she be normal? Being a vegan doesn't seem that political or humane. Why can't she protect dogs—"

"That's a long way down. Do you think the trains derailed and tumbled down these high edges?"

"I don't think they derail. But maybe."

"So you were saying about being humane."

"There are ways to fight for causes without hurting another being. She hurt me."

"I am sorry she hurt you."

When the man pulls into the apartment complex's main-office driveway, she exits his car and stands outside the gate. She and her father could not open the gate to their apartment complex because they lost the gate beeper. When her father went into the office to ask the landlord for a replacement, the landlord informed him that it would cost fifty dollars. So her father told her that they would just live without it, and hopefully in a few months they could move out. They waited until the gates were opened by their neighbors, who came in and out of the complex on a regular basis. Sometimes the wait time was only one minute and at other times, ten to fifteen minutes.

After the man drops her off, she roams the vacant streets of Vegas, moving from one establishment to the next. She doesn't leave of her own volition, but due to the insensitivity of the establishments' workers. Smith's closes at 1 a.m. but its franchised Starbucks is only open till 7 p.m. Hiding herself in the obscure corner of the Smith's Starbucks during post-closing hours, in a dark recess where light from the bright fresh fruits and vegetables and bakery can't reach her, she sits, watching YouTube videos of Lady Gaga, alone with her MacBook Pro, not disturbing a soul. But Smith's cashiers and staff have been noticing her ubiquitous nocturnal presence. And although she does not harass or hurt or even bother them, her esoteric, nonconforming, antihuman behavior is a sore on their eyes, and that evening a staff member, not a manager, approaches her in the darkness of Starbucks's one-person leather sofa to let her know she can't be here after 7 p.m. The staff members like to make fugacious rules, rules they invent overnight, designed just for her, when her abnormal behavior appears to threaten no one. It's as if those dark maple, wooden Starbucks chairs blocking the entrance to the café had been erected as a barricade to prevent her from entering, so that she couldn't sit down in the dark to watch Lady Gaga or the alcoholic flights of antiheroine Jessica Jones, her face, which gives off the glow of a neon sign, randomly haunting the staff member's waking hours, especially those insomniac hours when they couldn't shut off the master-bedroom light of their minds, when their minds won't shut down and they feel totally dead on the inside, not like zombies but like those stale, leftover French baguettes they are forced to discard every day into large gray garbage bins.

After being kicked out of Smith's, she roams the streets of Vegas again. It's 1 a.m. She has a home, but her shoulders walk like a homeless person, droopy and a little hunched. Her eyes search the streets for 24-7 grocery stores or gas stations or casinos. Turning her body to the left, she notices the empty parking lot of the night. To the right, blinking neon lights of gas stations and restaurants compete with the loneliness of the obscure, unblink-ing bright signs of other businesses. She desperately does not want to return home, despite feeling utterly exhausted. Her eyes are falling asleep and her mind isn't awake. But she is afraid to return home, to her father's place. She isn't afraid to confront him or even to be around him. She is afraid that she might forgive him. All he would need to do is smile or ask her if she has eaten. She has begun to see that forgiveness was reigniting the cycle of abuse. She does not want to forgive her father. A smile from him would be a killer.

A quarter of a mile from her father's place, she spots a pub, not hidden from public view, but hidden from her until now. In fact, the pub is a massive orange building and it has always been there, so close to her own home. The pub is open 24-7. She stands in front of its entrance and, when she finally decides to try to enter, finds it locked. A sign catches her eye. It says to use the buzzer if the gate is locked. She hesitates. Should she go home and share a bed with her father? And face the inevitable? Or should she roam the vacant streets some more, or should she push the buzzer that would let her in, where she would be physically safe but maybe not psychologically?

A buzzer clicks the gate open. To test-drive her intuition, the door is unlatched. And, true to her calm but not cautious sensibilities, she walks in. The dining area is as bright as day, but no one—not a single soul, no waitstaff—is around. The pub is divided into three sections. The first section has been converted into a restaurant, the second into a bar room, and the third into a party room. Everything has the appearance and energy of a David Lynch film—polychromatic and dark and sultry and sad and fatuous. She unlatches the door to her right and walks in. She doesn't want to order anything. At Smith's she'd eaten a carton of Cheerios and isn't hungry. She just wants to watch the rest of the Kristen Stewart interview on YouTube. But the waiter's persistence activates her guilt and she caves in. She orders the apple crumble with ice cream and asks if it is okay to use her laptop.

She watches Kristen Stewart's jittery legs in nine interviews. One with Ellen; one with Jimmy Fallon, in which they take turns wearing earphones while trying to guess each other's spoken words; one with Kelly Reichardt and the actresses from *Certain Women*; one with *Camp X-Ray* director Peter Sattler (that one is boring); one with *Vanity Fair* editor Krista Smith; one with Peter Travers; one with Juliette Binoche. And so on and so forth. When she watches these interviews, she studies Kristen Stewart's body language and discovers that Kristen's energy vibrates at a different frequency than that of anyone she has ever known.

Later that evening, when she climbs into bed, she masturbates while thinking of Kristen. Kristen Stewart isn't her type, but she could be her type, given time and understanding. She masturbates thinking about her because she wants to sow telepathic energy between them, the sexual thread as a portal or a gate in which she could use the unfathomable, cosmic vim between them to encourage their two souls to vibrate at the same frequency. She masturbates to force herself to fall asleep fast, but also to open the cosmic window of Kristen in her soul. Only time will tell if their souls will align. Only time will tell if her orgasm has been effective in achieving her future endeavors.

She knows that it's time to head home when she begins to watch the ten most attractive men in the world. When she sees Prince William on the list, she tosses her hands in the air and leaves the pub immediately. Omar Borkan Al Gala is sexy, but William? She also wants to see Godfrey Gao's name. She considers his name to be the most sexy name in the world.

Before she falls asleep, she wonders why Kristen Stewart isn't her type.

Before she leaves the pub, the waiter introduces himself and calls himself Brandon. He says that the next time she wants to enter, she can press the buzzer.

She wakes up early but forces herself to fall back asleep so the daylight hours of her existence extinguish fast—like a chronic smoker who wishes not to experience the luxurious nicotine aftertaste but just wants to greedily and rapidly suck in all the smoke in one long, castrated inhale. But her lungs do not have the capacity of a swimmer's, and after taking one or two small, intermittent breaths she is awake. Fearing that her father will return home from his night with his girlfriend and thus force the inevitable encounter, she takes the quickest shower in the world. When foam from the soap collects in large batches of frothy clouds around her ankles and ambuscades the existence of her feet, she knows that the stress of homelessness and the stress of being in her father's home have exponentially grown; hair falling out in elephantine amounts is a symbol of female impotence and has the potential to block the flow of water, the flow of life from the top of her head down to her feet. With the dexterity of her toes, she lifts the lightweight metal strainer from the bathtub manhole and moves it a few inches to the left so that foam, soap, and water can pass through without her hair adding another layer of sieve. Out of the shower, she pumps the bottle of lotion, but nothing comes out. She presses all of her weight onto it, but not one drip. She nearly loses her balance putting all of her effort into it, but catches herself by clinging to the towel bar near the mirror at the last second. She notices a pair of red scissors leaning in a jar, and she uses them to cut the lotion bottle in half so she

can apply its insignificant dribble of lotion onto her skin, already
desiccated from the brutal dryness of the Vegas air. Despite the
pump's inability to reach the remote regions of the bottle's cor-
ners, there is still a significant amount of lotion left, enough to
cover her entire body. Cautiously, she opens the bathroom door,
fearing that her father may have returned already, but the silence
and darkness of the kitchen confirm otherwise. Naked, she opens
the kitchen drawer near the refrigerator, and in one short, swift
motion, she wraps the cut lotion bottle with polyvinyl chloride
to prevent air from solidifying it. This extra step will allow her
to use the remaining lotion for another day. She tosses the cut
container into the large drawer of the bathroom cabinet and gets
dressed.

In the evening, she walks out of her apartment complex and
comes face to face with a fluffy terrier. It does not have a leash
or a collar and appears to be lost and ownerless. She stares at it
for at least a minute. The dog does not move and reciprocates
her stare. It continues to stare at her until she begins to cross the
street. It leaps in the air in an attempt at fake excitement for its
existence and then, mimicking her, it crosses the street without looking to the left or right. It crosses the busy intersection
mindlessly and a truck plunges forward. To her, it appears as if
the dog has been squashed or flattened under the truck's wheels.
The truck comes to a halt. There is massive confusion and the
traffic stops. A surprise to her, the furry animal emerges from
beneath the truck. It appears uninjured, or it appears injured
but hyper and so gives off the appearance of no injury. It runs all
about while cars stop in the midst of the traffic. The hyper dog
runs toward the traffic light and a woman gets out of her truck
to chase after it as it runs quickly away from her. While all traffic
halts on behalf of the dog and on behalf of her running after it,

she catches up to the dog, curls it into her arms, and walks back to her truck. The driver, her husband, drives off once she enters with the dog in her arms.

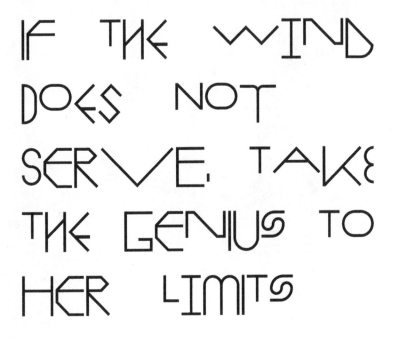

IF THE WIND DOES NOT SERVE, TAKE THE GENIUS TO HER LIMITS

She has been spending a lot of time at Starbucks eating cereal.

The baristas leave her alone. At night, five minutes before closing, they tell her that they will be closing in five minutes. By the end of the first week, they no longer use words to say they are closing. She meets the gaze of the baristas and they nearly open their mouths, but they don't.

The reason why she eats Cheerios is because they have only

two grams of sugar. Everything in life tastes too sweet to her. Everywhere she goes. Even asphalt tastes too much of dextrose, dripping with artificial honey and sugar. Whenever she walks, the earth seems to glue her to its soil. It takes all of her power and force to pull herself together to move forward.

She has just left Panda Express after ordering a small entree of grilled teriyaki chicken with sauce on the side. She knows the sauce is molasses on a bed of honey on a bed of sorghum on a bed of agave.

When she sits down to pull the chicken from its carton with a pair of chopsticks at Starbucks, she notices the server's name on the receipt: Nicole with a Y. Nycole. She originally thought the server was Mexican, with a face of barbacoa, not a white girl whose mother, when pregnant with her, took handfuls of Tylenol.

That evening, she tries to use the Starbucks bathroom stall but it is occupied. It remains occupied for another hour. Ten minutes before closing, she notices a tall white boy with thin hair exiting. His hair is wet, as if he has glued patches of hay on it to make it look human-like. He has taken a sink-based shower at Starbucks. He is wearing a new pair of jeans and an off-white T-shirt. They are wrinkled and it makes his articles appear old and dirty and soiled. When he turns his face, his eyes look like a rattlesnake's— one that is born in the cold, swirling its body across the desert where undocumented Mexicans emigrate so their labor can be exploited.

For hours, sitting in a corner near a colored photograph of un-ripe cherries in a mahogany wood frame, a young man wearing a gray sweater has been on a business call. She assumes the person on the other end is a woman, because it takes him a while to quote the estimate of a service. He assures her that he would pay well. He is willing to pay $500 for two days work. Work that isn't homemade vadouvan. His rental isn't French colonial.

While watching David Chang refusing to eat donkey meat on episode 5 of his *Ugly Delicious*, she hears the businessman saying loudly, "I don't want to be the middleman. I want to be the boss. Either step up or leave. Exactly. Exactly. I am not going to beg someone to go. Does that make sense? I probably would say to him, 'Hey, you are probably not ready for this, man. He hasn't. He hasn't.' Give me some room to think and make some phone calls."

David Choe, the street artist, who chooses payment in Facebook shares and has a non-liquid asset worth of between 1/5 and 1/2 billion dollars, tries donkey meat for the first time in Korea. The meat is ranked 2nd after dragon, which doesn't technically exist.

"Because of the shorter lease? I don't know what to say. What-ever. Gotcha. Are you doing it on your own either way? Let me take you off this list. I will be there Wednesday, Thursday, Friday. I'll see you."

"What's up, buddy. Trying to set up the housing. When is your date of arrival? That's what I was thinking, too. And, then. Okay. I am working on the housing. For the first week, we will do hotels. Let me walk you through it. It's a weekly rent. A single. A room you share with someone. $125 a week and a private place that is smaller. Let's do that. Okay. That's up to you. It's up to you. If you have a car, you can drive here. Basically, most likely, you most likely. Most mobile option. Yeah. It comes with a new bed. New dresser. So everything is new. You can buy it here. And then pots, pans, and stuff, and some cheap stuff. Perfect. Perfect. Oh. Cool. Oh, no. It's all me. I just need a date and time. Yeah. I can commit for a summer without being everywhere. How much is the flight? I'll come back with something. Yeah. Yeah. Southwest. Sounds good. Appreciate it. Thanks."

A newspaper sitting across from him, abandoned on a high metal chair, announces the death of 76-year-old Linda Brown, who was the center of the 1954 Supreme Court decision to end public school segregation. He is white and does not care. He wants his menu and his ammunitions to rent. Because the newspaper is made of paper, and has not crossed the dangerous, gelid desert to be here, the barista won't deport it. At least not until the end of the day. At the end of the day, she'll toss it into a garbage bin.

There are others, those who know how to make non-Arab-style tacos so well, with chicken chicharron and salsa mocha and coconut fat and ginger, who are banned from the United States for life.

And so she hears, not like bleached broccoli deep fried in chicken fat would sound:

"Hey. How fast can you get the menu done? I am trying to get the housing done. Do I need to write a letter? Can we get the stuff all go? Call Chris. What is the target we are trying to shoot for? Yeah. Let's get it done today. Oh, yeah. I am not mad at anybody. Alright. Shoot me."

The barista passes by her to inform a man in his early forties that they are closing in five. He turns to her, "But your website says you close at 10 p.m."

"Our hours changed."
He gives her the kind of gaze one would give a crawfish, a Viet-Cajun crawfish. In one swift mental gesture he could decapitate her and suck all of her hepatopancreas and membranes out. In his mind, he is breaking her antennas, her central nervous system, her receptor cells.

She walks away and begins to sweep an area that requires little to no sweeping.

When the five minutes pass, the patron approaches the transparent exit door. He points to the hours sign. "It says 10 p.m. 10 p.m! I'm not joking!"

He leaves, then he screams to the nocturnal Vegas air: "If the wind will not serve, take the genius to her limits!"

"Foie gras, mudbugs, paprika, and butter are transcendent mistresses of the tongue—who am I to question the stucco, U-shaped ranch of Starbucks's operational hours? Who am I to crave foie gras?" The patron shouts and shouts these words.

"If Starbucks would operate their businesses as stated on their website and at their business locations, I wouldn't be so crazy. I just wouldn't. I just wouldn't."

He climbs into his black Volkswagen Jetta sedan. In the dark, it's hard to tell that it's handsome. The dealer had informed him that it's subcompact, but having owned it for nearly three months, he thinks this is inaccurate.

He lives in the information age. The information highway always kicks him off, always asks him to de-emerge, always kicks him off the ramp.

After he turns on the engine, he pummels the steering wheel with his fists.

"It's not fair. It's simply not fair."

He backs his sedan out of the Starbucks's parking lot. Once he gets on the highway, he drives really fast. Thirty miles per hour over the speed limit. Even for Vegas, it is fast. Everyone here drives fast and wicked. They drive the way they gamble. Except for the gunman. The gunman knew the rules of gaming and taking chances.

Just five minutes into his semi-manic driving, red lights flash in circular motions behind him. He pulls over and a tall police officer climbs out of his car and walks towards him.

"Do you know how fast you were driving?"
"Starbucks closed at 9 p.m. when it says 10 on their main door."
"Your license and registration please."
"Starbucks closed at 9 p.m. It says 10 on their website."
"Your license and registration please."
"Starbucks closed at 9 p.m. when it says 10 on their main door."
"Have you been drinking?"
"Starbucks closed at 9 p.m. when it says 10 on their website. Starbucks doesn't serve alcohol."
"Your license and registration please."

"Starbucks closed at 9 p.m. when it says 10 on their main door."
"I'm going to have to ask you to step out of the car, sir!" the police officer barks.
"If the wind will not serve, take the genius to her limits."
"Sure."
"My vocal cord is the genius. Not my driving!"
"Step out of the car now!" the police officer orders.
"I think I'm wrong here. I don't think it's my vocal cord. Do you think it's my vocal cord?"

A talented young poet in a writing program once told her, "I used to grow the nail on my pinky so that whenever I ate crawfish I could dig all of the meat out. I love crawfish, man. I just love it. I just don't like it when there are leftovers. Do you know what I mean? Even if it's hidden."

THE UZI COULD BE A LANDSCAPE OF LOVE

The wonderful pimp tells her before she leaves Vegas.

THE PIMP: It's just a camouflage! It's just a camouflage.
   When she tells you she wants it slow: it's just a camouflage.
   One of you got to make the move.
DAFFODIL: It had better not be me, because I have been
   okay with complacency. She had not been okay with com-
   placency.

She thinks about the futility of it all. Kingston had been so busy.
Though there were blankets of time when she could milk or

nourish the lightbulb of her desire. There was no going nowhere with this. She knew meeting her would be futile, but she wanted to anyway.

She was in the middle of New York, and Kingston was at a boutique hotel in Lower Eastside.

Middle of Manhattan. Raining. Steam blowing steam from all the high towers and chimneys of skyscrapers. Even fog couldn't tell itself from steam.

Was it the glances between the two women? Or was there too much swimming pool around them, where people jumped and didn't die? She could jump, but she wouldn't die. What gave her body away? Her desire?

Daffodil had told her friend, A, that when she opened, Kingston also opened. Then she scared her away by telling her how passionate she was. Thus, Kingston closed herself off. In response, she closed too, fearing abandonment and torture. Time passed and they met again. Kingston reopened but, conflicted by the memory of pain, she closed and inadvertently forced Kingston to close too. Time passed. She has been so lonely. Her loneliness is stronger than her fear of risk and love and she stands up straight to walk around the penthouse and thinks, loneliness hurts, fear of intimacy hurts. Everything hurts. If something has to hurt, she might as well enjoy the journey.

She calls her friend A, who tells her to love from her own point of view. One could never know what others think or feel or how they will behave.

DAFFODIL: This is the time to make a move. She is open and
I am open too. We are both open.

Daffodil asks A to psychoanalyze Kingston based on her recent
novel, so that she could be Napoleon and see the battle plan of
love, and whether she had any chance of not winning the war.
No, she hasn't expected to win the war. She hasn't expected to
win one battle. But she wanted, at least, to cross the enemy's
line before being pummeled back to dust. Once she crossed the line,
she knew she would be the first to enter the battle arena and she
knew that if she had to die, she would be reborn into a person, a
person who was a superior version of herself, not necessarily better, just a lateral move across the 4th dimension of her existence
where ontology is still ontology and knowledge is still knowledge. The 5th dimension is where ontology becomes oncology.
And knowledge is having as many prostitutes as you like.

DAFFODIL: I am in K's penthouse, talking to you. Based
on her recent novel, tell me please what kind of lover she
would be.
A: I read her a few months ago. There is intensity to her writing.
DAFFODIL: I worry my passion and intensity will upset her.
A: I get the sense that Kingston and you would balance each
other out.

Daffodil gets the message: she could handle my intensity, if I
myself am intense.

Her wonderful friend who was a pimp could be right. This is just
a camouflage. Kingston's fear could camouflage another kind of
fear: fear of goggles. Daffodil does not wear goggles. But wisdom

is a kind of nocturnal optic. She would see through the fog and darkness and reveal the essence of the essence. She wouldn't be a danger to herself and her Uzi would just be a formality, romantically.

A: Yes, based on her writing, there is intensity there."

Kingston informs her that she must see her mother. She heads to Oregon, the first state to ban Blacks, in 1844.

Nothing could protect Kingston from the loneliness of her choice. She made a choice, justified by some degree of logic and some degree of friendship. There are consequences measured by the end spectrum of loneliness. It has been a long day made short by a long nap she didn't intend on taking, but that had taken her. The nap waited to take her. It has caught up to her and even when she smelled desire leaping off her nodding heart, she pushed it out like she pushes waves back into the sea. The waves have woken her from desire and reminded her that love is painful and that she shouldn't go there too soon. She has been pushing desire away from her even when her body is in conflict with her past. She hasn't been held by a woman in so long. She recalls a time when an apple had been peeled off, naked, exuding a fragrance of citrus, but was left on the kitchen counter to rot into loneliness. Devoid of the embrace of the hand or the mouth or a naked bowl, just like she herself, sitting in the hotel lobby, admiring a bonsai tree whose height is shorter than all her pumps lined up in a row in her hotel room like the crooked teeth of a stranger. When the stranger opened his mouth wide, she saw yesterday swollen like a crushed pregnant bird. She had come from somewhere near, a suburb of a large city known for its steak and the best ice cream in the world. Sitting in front of the expectedly abbreviated bonsai, she finds herself alone and lonely amongst her friends. Standing behind her are future customers of the hotel, and lining up before her are five hotel receptionists wearing wrapping-paper bowties. After all, she has made a decision to put responsibility, life, and friendship above the law of love. Love has hurt her badly. Even when she tries to pull love back into her arms, it resists her. Love arrives to her when she sits at a fine dinning restaurant with her colleagues after spending long, vacant conference hours disputing the claims her clients made about having to replenish toilet paper at a timeshare station. Love slips out of the door to eat kimchee with a food truck.

She made her life busy by not focusing on love.

She knows better now than to ask a straight woman for advice on homosexual love.

She notices a pattern is forming and she wants to cut its pre-hydra heads off before they have the opportunity to grow.

The woman is trying to cockblock her, has been trying to cockblock her. She has been effective. She has been cockblocking herself. The memory of pain can do that to you. Just as imagining the future can do that to you.

> A: You have no option but to be interested in yourself. I am interested in your growth, and where this growth will lead you. When you explore her by being vulnerable, your interest grows.
> DAFFODIL: We haven't had our first kiss yet. I want to be gentle and assertive, but not aggressive.
> A: The opposite of aggression is being open.

DAFFODIL: I haven't thought of it that way.

A: You are not aggressive because you are open. Being passive is not considering yourself enough, and being aggressive means you have no consideration for others. You must voice your possibilities. Your impossibility is born through avoiding knowing yourself. You cannot know yourself through others. One way to know yourself well is by being vulnerable. Are you in love?

DAFFODIL: Not yet.

A: The courtship has been slow. Very slow.

Love is love. Loneliness is loneliness.

So Daffodil texts Kingston: Make time; share the rain with me.

She waits for hours for her to reply while the rain slips down the curtain of glass. The skyscrapers populate and pollute her view of the world.

Did she mean to say: share the pain with me?

Daffodil has shut off the light inside herself. She has shut down the streams of rain, the body of movement associated with thieves of time and of the undesirable. Love isn't a disguise or concealment. Love is a person, an animal, or an object, but not God.

By opening, she would have the opportunity to let go and be less aggressive. By closing, she is stuck in limbo and her decision is paralyzed by logic traps. By closing, she is forced to regret.

THE HUMAN CAMOUFLAGE

Nothing can protect you from loneliness. Not even your friends who have the best intentions in the world. Not even the ones who love you so much and are so near you; even if they breathe and exist in the same house or apartment complex as you. Nothing protects you, lost in the sea of bobbing human heads, piles of dirt, finely combed grass, and blaring bright headlights. You are at an intersection, caught between despair and destruction of self. You don't know how to even begin.

You have been so alone for so long, even your body sobs in between metro stops and you turn around in your loneliness, which has become a devastation, like a natural disaster, but an individual natural disaster, without the natural, and everyone's eyes are inside themselves, inside the moving tube of the tunnel gazing into the dumb ceiling of their empty imagination, not paying any attention or heed to you and why should they pay any heed. You are nobody. You have been nobody for so long, even longer than your aging Canadian whiskey. You have been so frustrated with yourself, not knowing how to convert your de-humanization, your deconstruction of self, your humiliation into a body capable of love.

In the past you valued friendship above everything else. Your friends have meant so much to you, more valuable than gold. You applauded yourself for being a great friend. Discarding your lovers on the side of the road for your friendships. You think your lover or your partner is important, but not that important. You proceed towards life like a flower that needs fertilizer, but not soil. But your friends, in their fleshly beauty, need no gold to protect their agency of being. They can open their refrigerators and their refrigerators are not empty. Your refrigerator is always empty. Maybe there is a glass of milk half-sought by your lips. They are who they are: candles blown in the wind, expiring with a slight breeze. The monsters inside you have been torched by snow.

But who will protect you when you are sitting in a beautiful apartment with your beautiful new sofa and your ice cream maker and your dance studio? You are surrounded by opulence and beauty and cleanliness and you are sad all over. Even your body can't forgive you for being this alone. It begs for tenderness and the unbearable caress of dyad breaths. Your friends can't protect you when you are this clean.

You come home to nobody. Where are your friends now—when you have infinity sitting by you like a second skin? Who will protect you? Where will you go? Who do you breathe next to? You may find yourself burning in hell for the virtue of being there for a friend. The tasteless, futile sacrifice you made because it felt honorable, but became hellish later. Your friends with their blissful partners do not understand or know. Why should they?

They did not make the choice to abandon their partners; they made the choice to abandon you. You did not know any better, because you had been known as the honorable one. The one who would not choose her lovers over her friends. But you are alone now, ashamed and lost and sobbing uncontrollably.

You are merely a verb not recorded. When you were a noun, nobody cared.

How often do we choose ephemerality over permanence because it looks more compelling in the moment?

Why do we dance with darkness and sadness when we could dance with light?

We take for granted how easily time changes her radio station. And we take for granted how wonderful it is and how necessary it is to have a human comforter, a human table cloth, a human psyche, dancing to the tune of another human psyche, a human chair, a human toilet seat, a human mirror, a human pillowcase, a human chopstick, a human sweater, a human body heater, a human bathrobe, a human scarf, a human sofa, a human chef, a human book, a human gaze, a human breath machine.

YOUR SADNESS IS SALT ON SALT

Your sadness is salt on salt. Your mind is broth, a cup of soup oversalted, so that whenever you taste your memory, you're thinking, ARTESIAN, you become oversalted, like your mind has been eating and sipping too much broth of the sea. Your tongue aches. Everything aches. You begin to wonder why everything, even something as sweet as a watermelon, tastes so salty. You ponder and ponder, overworking your tongue. You begin to recalibrate your mind's taste buds. You begin to taste the real flavor of life. The taste of life is rich and complex; you can taste every single molecule. You want sadness to not consume your entire tongue, the broth pot of your body and life. You begin to have more protean emotions, happiness and verve and enthusiasm which had walked away from your mouth long ago. You begin to feel again, to feel the tiny saplings of love regrowing in a forest fire you believed you had caused. Everything you had once created burnt away in that fire. You open your eyes and ears to the new salt, and maybe to the umami, hiding in the cauliflower bush beside the sidewalk that walks on the soles of your feet. You sway like a hammock in the desert wind. Your tongue radiates life into new clusters of nerve so that all the nerve endings in your tongue attach themselves to new atoms of light and you begin to taste life again, the way you first swam into the world, a fish fighting for your own breath and life. You are a fish swimming in a pot of well-seasoned broth, your fish eyes shimmering with radiant mercury, liquid temperature languishing with tiny salt pulses. Your tongue licks the liquid mercury, gray and at the mercy of your infinite taste buds. You can eat you if you like, or you can share yourself with someone else. But you are you and you sit at the center of a banquet; those who eat you will never want to eat anything else. This is your new life. You begin your new abundance right away.

FIELD NOTES ON SUICIDE OR THE INABILITY TO COMMIT SUICIDE or IT'S HARD TO FOLLOW A POMERANIAN AROUND

She has overstayed her welcome at Starbucks.

Starbucks closed at 10 pm. At 10:05 pm, she found herself approached by an impatient barista. The barista opened her mouth.

"We are closed."
"I know."

She finds her body parked outside Starbucks, at its incongruent parameter, near an un-threatening short cactus just shorter than her knees. She stood there gazing at the nocturnal, desolate traffic of the sinful but sinless city. Everything was sprawled out, including the air and its cars. People had already rushed home to eat their saturated-fat dinners with take-out burgers, fries, and decadent donuts, and to pre-pad their tummies with carbohydrate-dense pad thais. The lonesomeness of her existence makes the desolate landscape before her ache with desiccated, nocturnal residuum.

Time passes through her and around her.

At the parameter, she cries for three hours. When she cries, the wind is strong and her tears flutter away from her horizontally. The tears flutter like a scarf, ready to wrap themselves around the throat of Sin City, strangling it if they could. They are the kind of tears that are migratory and soundless. The city sleeps through her lachrymal profundity. The city won't let her commit suicide. She walks through a million different versions of how she could die or want to die.

Is it sinful to be trampled by a mini-van, by two adults on their way to the Bellagio to see the fountain dance the night away?

How does a person watch a city commit suicide and then get raped?

While climbing a small hill in New Mexico, another woman narrated to her a story about a dog who was kidnapped and raped in Mexico City. Her abductors wanted her to multiply their profits by forcing her to give birth, but her menstrual cycle hadn't arrived yet, at least not inside her body, and she was unable to reproduce. The abductors were in a hurry. The dog's owner had stapled reward pamphlets around the city and the abductors, how clever, returned the violated dog to the owner and she, in irony, gave the reward money to the abductors.

How does a city find itself amongst the different narrative structures of the city?
With which building should it ambush or clothe its soul?
When a city doesn't clothe itself in the nightmares of the past, what must a person who wishes to commit suicide but can't do?

A city sprawled out, waiting for a pamphlet to kiss it.
A city within a city, crawling around, wanting a good fuck.
Who is willing to fuck it?
Will it have any good luck?

Sin City will tell you all about it. About its time sleeping with Donald Trump, Steve Wynn, Andre Agassi, Jenna Jameson, Chelsie Hightower, and Stevenson Sylvester.

A tennis ball rolls down a hill. Its path is dictated by gravity, not volition. The violation is in its silence, once the ball loses its kinetic momentum when the city doesn't turn its hips or shoulders or its arms so the ball could accelerate more. Its volition is in its silence, not its resilience. Who is capable of destroying whom?

"I was a camel owner before I was a dog owner," says the desert
as it watches the child of Mexico City rape a dog. The desert
is not a rolling tongue. In the heat, wetness is a luxury, which
the tongue can afford but not the landscape. There are myriad
ways to intellectualize, to culturalize, to educate momentum and
human velocity (not ball velocity). The ferociousness of a blind
tennis ball.

The human spirit rolls down a city, with or without gravity or
momentum. Its enemy isn't the tennis ball. Its enemy is itself.
Its enemy is the climate of change, which climbs the backs of all
mountain lions. At night, the wind howls and cries and even the
human spirit gets weathered and weakened by the sound of the
city dumbed-down by sinless gambling and tactless cocktails. She
cries in front of the city, her back to Starbucks.

Is it luck or is it noise that she considers suicide? It is not her last
resort. Her last resort is to return home. To climb into bed. To
enter an empty apartment without fish sauce inside.

An inferior soul is a soul that decides to change its shirt from
blue to white after a change of climate.

An inferior soul is an Impala after it pulls out of the driveway
of a house that has spent a night sleeping in the cremation of a
dream.

An inferior soul is a bottle of water that has withdrawn its mem-
bership from a watermelon orchard.

A superior soul knows when it is winter and when it will snow.

Outside, the mud remembers a young dog, a pomeranian, who
ran away from Iran because somewhere in its heritage is the
Caspian Sea and the Persian gulf, with a population of approxi-
mately 66 million, not dog population.

Before 1979, Iran was a monarchy.
Before 1979, the young pomeranian was the progeny of a rapist.
Before 1979, was there an Iranian in a pomeranian?
So began the Iran-Iraq War.
And then in 2001, the US got involved in a very romantic rela-
tionship with a fake nuclear psychoanalyst called Afghanistan.
A superior soul knows when to adopt an Iranian pomearanian
and how to not start a deja-vu-esque, quasi, post-repetitive Viet-
nam War with the Middle East.

Outside, a water pump is in the midst of being built, and maybe
a gas station that sells Doritos.

Meanwhile, a rose bush is manually lit on fire.

And Moses tells Aaron that he is hired to be his own White
House correspondent and the Sea God asks him to part its
non-nuclear weapon, i.e. technology. Facebook, mainly.

PART 2

WHEN THE MEMORY FOAM MATTRESS REFUSES TO BECOME THE NEXT PRESIDENT OF THE UNITED STATES

October's cyber lover is more concrete than some of her other, nondigital acquaintances. Acquaintances she could hug and even concretely deceive if she wanted to, but she is not one to want deception. She likes living in the moment and the best way to live in the moment is to tell the truth. She tells the truth, but in a way that makes those around her suffer. This is counterintuitive to the design of veracity. Though is veracity the design? Or does she want the design to operate a certain way? There are times when their intimacy is so strong and compelling, she feels as if her cyber lover could impale distance or shatter the inflexible shape of physical reality. Sometimes when they are sexting, October feels an overwhelming desire to move through walls like a ghost before arriving to her lover like a bedsheet cover on a mattress. In this world, life does not pass slowly. In fact, it does not pass at all. Obscene and extraordinary intimacy can defy and obliterate distance and space.

October wakes in Vegas. The light has been so bright; it keeps her from falling asleep. She imagines her cyber lover driving from DC to Brooklyn to see an ex who had chosen to leave her cyber lover three months ago. It's a four-hour drive. Her cyber lover, CL, wants to fuck her ex and maybe transform their relationship into one of friendship. A week ago they had fought over this. CL just wants to date and so does she; to see where it goes; to give herself permission to explore instead of committing fatally to the first woman she lays eyes on. It makes sense. On paper. Over the digital space that separates the two of them. But their intimacy has grown obscenely fast. Almost fatally fast. Although it seems right, there is also something not right about it.

CL felt it was unethical or not right to keep hidden her desire for an ex in Brooklyn and the potential of fucking. And so, when October wakes up in the bright light of Sin City, she feels a throb in her cunt, like a heartbeat in a second heart. The throbbing is visceral. She can't think of anything to do but to be with it. She could easily touch herself and climax, but her body is responding to a death and rebirth of some kind. Throbbing viscerally is her cunt's way of expressing its philosophical stance on immortality. Immorality relies much on death to be more of itself. Especially in an era when time travels at the speed of light.

She remembers CL declaring, "I haven't lied through omission. I need time to get to know you before I reveal the details of my past." October had felt protective of her, of her saying that omission is sometimes the truth addressed in reverse, a way of slowing time down, to keep it from panting behind the heels of her heart.

When CL informs her about potentially sleeping with an ex, October withdraws immediately. She has shifted into a self-protective mode. Her cyber lover responds viscerally, feeling the intimacy between them shifting towards superficiality; it feels threatening, and they began to fight as if they had been together for a decade. But they had only met twelve days ago. Their relationship was still open, open for others to explore inward. Open for casual sex and for micro-depths of despair.

Her CL continues to court her, but October remains ambivalently cold, wanting to be closer but fearing the betrayal of that closeness.

One night, CL sexts her after a long day of research and reading. October rebuts her. She isn't moved by the foreplay. She shuts down and withdraws. After several nights of fighting over the sexting, CL begins to withdraw as well. Loneliness and hard work consume her long, sleepless day. CL continues to express tenderness towards October, and each time she does she is moved, but she does not tell CL. She does not reveal to CL that she has spent long afternoons thinking about her and masturbating three or four times a day.

When she wakes up, her cunt throbs. Go back to sleep, she tells her cunt. I need to sleep this afternoon away, she tells her cunt. But her cunt is a dog who barks at her and wants to be fed. She thinks of CL and flares of electrodes take her out of bed into the kitchen. She is awoken with massive desire and yearning. She imagines CL kissing the base of her neck, holding her in her arms, wrapping her arms around her like a bedsheet. She is overwhelmed with inescapable desire for her cyber lover.

CL, struggling to sleep after a long, strenuous day of work, expresses her desire for a cheese sandwich and talks about how lonely and hungry she was. The expression of vulnerability shatters the wall of October's coldness. She offers to read poetry to help CL fall asleep. During the reading, her desire for CL grows like a small sapling that wishes to become an ancient oak tree overnight. She lets it grow inside her silently and quietly. The use of the word "let" is inaccurate; she has no choice but to feel overwhelming tenderness for CL, and she tells herself that she would be open and not resentful about CL sleeping with her ex. In fact, she wants CL to have the opportunity to experience physical intimacy and tenderness from her ex. If they fuck, perhaps she will feel less lonely and less hungry. Ultimately, she wants CL to be happy. If fucking her ex makes her happy or temporarily relieves her from loneliness or hunger, she wants that for CL. She begins to think of ways to give CL guilt-free permission to do so. But how? Without seeming to donate her cyber lover to another, but rather as an expression of her tenderness and warmness for CL.

Originally she'd wanted CL to save it for her. After all, she hasn't fucked anyone for 17 months. She wants it to be special between them. But she can't demand this from her new cyber lover whom she hasn't even met. But, as she learns rather quickly, she could request it. Learning to ask is a new vocabulary, a language she finds uncomfortable. But she is willing. So she begins to say, "If I am saving it for our encounter...." She fails to ask the obvious, "Will you save it for me?" A part of her doesn't want to communicate the obvious because she wants CL to desire it, to save it, the fucking, that is, for their encounter, and she wants CL to want to do it without her asking. Her ideal lover is someone who senses what she needs and gives it to her before she even asks for it.

October imagines her cyber lover fucking her ex and welcoming it with all her heart. It seems more than okay and surely why not. It doesn't diminish her tenderness or her growing intimacy for CL. In fact, the idea of giving her lover what she wants seems like a loving thing. She fears, though, that when they fight, she will question about why CL didn't save the fucking for her. It's this micro, pre-charged emotion that concerns her the most. So, in order to protect the future of their love and prevent future fights, not encouraging CL to fuck her ex seems like the wisest and most giving choice of all. An investment that can't be seen in the immediate future but in the future of all futures. That relentless happiness is available between CL and her; such happiness can find them. October wants CL to make that choice and if she doesn't, perhaps CL isn't the right person for her and it will all work well in the end. She wonders if CL is willing to forgo a few fucking nights with her ex for something great between her and CL.

Only time will tell. Meanwhile, seven school-children were stabbed to death in northern China and post-bullying stress disorders can leave many open exit wounds on the body of porn star Stormy Daniels, who may have received a paycheck of $130,000 so that her silence would reveal nothing more than the affair she had with Trump.

THE VEGAS DILEMMA

It's 81 degrees in the heat of the sun. Death has barely made her daily measure, yet the sun refreshes its refulgent thirst on her. On her skin. On her coat. On her gleaming face filled with dark shadows cast by the stubborn bright light. She is wearing a green hoody with metal buttons from Hollister. Over her hoody is a dress coat the color of the post-industrial revolution and beneath all of these warm layers is a black turtleneck. The turtleneck is to absorb the electromagnetic radiation if everything else fails, if the sun could penetrate deep into the depth of her coat's thread count and through the different textile division centers of Hollister.

Life has tied her hands behind her back with the rope of credit. She can't even impulsively fly to DC or Baltimore. She needs kidney facility with 63. A second expresso. The Drought of Francophile. And all the magnetic fields of assholes and fuckers and coffee belts alike. The way a shopping cart fell into the ravine. Bushy green cacti strangling the shopping cart, latching onto it like ivy vines across brick walls.

In New Mexico, she learns very quickly why the cashier walks her to the parking lot, waits for her to open her trunk, empty the groceries into the trunk, and then walks back to the store with the cart.

Shopping carts are costly. It costs the store $200 per shopping cart lost either through abandonment or embezzlement or home-less folks who walk away with it because they are homeless and they want the shopping cart to be homeless too. In New Mexico, the population is poor. Not damaged poor. But hyperallergically poor and shopping cart friendly. At first, she thinks the cashier is chivalrous like a walrus (gregarious and with downward-point-ing tusks, ready to de-vein all of her suitors if they were to come for her with severe verve). The cashier is escorting her to her car like a date, ready to open the door to her Impala. But chivalry is often dressed as anti-theft fiscal responsibility, designed to melt the hearts of grocery stores' bank accounts. This kind of chivalry is not ladylike or like gentlemen in high heels.

She walks with her head down. She wants to prevent the light from penetrating her and from turning her into an anti-sun-screen advertisement. She prefers billboards: they are larger and seem so visually verbal on the long highways.

A man finds her by accident. He comes out of nowhere to greet her. He is black as night. And black as black. And he is her friend.

He approaches her.

A: "Girl, why are you wearing a hoody? In this bloody heat?"

Q: "It protects me from the sun."

A: "What about a cap or a hat?"

Q: "It will blow in the wind."

A: "There is no wind today!"

Q: "There was last night."

A: "You gotta wear something that doesn't make you look dangerous."

Q: "I look dangerous?"

A: "People will think you look crazy. In this heat and the hoody. And your winter jacket."

Q: "I get cold easily."

A: "The cops haven't arrested you yet or attacked you?"

Q: "No, not yet."

A: "It's dangerous to wear a hoody."

Q: "But I like hoodies. They don't get blown in the wind."

A: "You should wear a baseball cap or something."

Q: "Did you hear about Starbucks?"

A: "Yes."

Q: "She'll never get a job again."

A: "It's really too bad."

Q: "She'll need to rely on her family now for income."

A: "No one would want to hire her."

Q: "What was she thinking?"

A: "It wasn't racial. It's never racial."

Q: "What do you mean?"

A: "She was having a bad day. Probably something happened to her before she came to work. And instead of leaving her problems at home, she took them to work with her. By the time she realized what she had done when she called the police, it was too late. She couldn't undo it. This is why people can't bring their issues to work. You have to be professional about it. You can't take things with you."

Q: "Something happened to her at home and she brought it to work. She was just reacting to something bad at home?"

A: "That's right. It's never about race. She didn't just come to work and say 'today, I will be a racist.'"

Q: "It is a human experience."

A: "Those guys are millionaires now. They have their lawyers now. Black power—knowing when to make use of it."

Q: "Probably the easiest money they ever made."

A: "The thing is…"

Q: "What thing?"

A: "Don't you know that blacks run this country? Look at basketball, football, baseball—we run this fucking country!"

Man invents photography in order to explain the origin of the universe. Man takes lots and lots of pictures. Until he finds the perfect one to display on National Geographic. God has been taking photographs by the millions, trying out the different cosmic takes on reality. His photos have been ugly in the most beautiful way possible. Take a look at Pluto or Saturn for instance. Earth has been God's National Geographic. How many photos did he take in order to get us there? To make the perfect condition for the survival of beauty? God in the dark room of the cosmos, developing planets. Look at his color photographs. Aren't they something?

Later that night he texts her a dick pic, a long black dick. It is ugly. They exchange the following text messages:

Q: What are you doing?

A: I haven't been home. I, at Starbucks. You?

Q: It's too late to be out walking. I have internet. Next time, ask me.

A: Thanks.

Q: They keep messaging me about how I won free books on Amazon

A: Lol. You can block them.

Q: Ok next time you show me how.

A: Yes.

Q: Ok. About to watch a girl on girl movie LOL

A: Lol. Enjoy. Don't get too excited

Q: Only 9½-inch excitement

A: Only

Q: I need to write a sex book

A: You do?

Q: The dame saves a cowboy and rides my horse

A: Hope it be a best seller

Q: I should have been a porn star

Q: How do I send my big black dick to Kavanaugh?

A: Who is he?

Q: I don't know. But he is just a T and a while away from being naughty.

A: I thought it was a drink that calms you. Like Kava tea.

Q: He is the opposite of calm. In the future, I predict he will be belligerent. All white men in power are belligerent. I thought Lindsey Graham was a woman, but he ain't no woman.

A: Is he a cracked walnut trapped in a republican?

Q: No. No. No! Trapped in Putin!

FOOTBALL BETS OUT OF STATE

She laughs a hysterical laugh with her back towards her. She tosses her hair from side to side to deride the doubt generated by the gloaming light between her thighs. Starfish and starfish. Pregnant with smartassness. She sits with her full body leaning forward. Fucking an idea without any idea.

Her annoyance is abundant and worth twelve days. The river in Iowa. Regular drinks. You'll like it as he touches her thighs. Flirtatious. Screaming at me. I like you and I want to hold your hand.

In a black dress, she crosses and uncrosses her legs. She doesn't want him to touch her but she is from North Dakota. You are the worst. She refuses him. You are the worst, he keeps repeating.

She is out of place. She works for men who live far away and can't come regularly. She makes football bets for them. They pay her well.

How well? she asks.
Very well.

Come here real quick. Something is wrong with her bra strap.
She keeps playing with it even though it is not falling. Keno is
ready to be cashed out. High heels so tall she is forced to use the
bathroom. The heels make her hipbone crooked and her bladder
too sensitive.

Royal flush.
Straight flush.

Bite my tongue. Shrimps in a little basket, he kept on saying.

She bursts into another hysterical laugh, as if to compensate for
the imbalance created by her obnoxious presence. She laughs,
ignoring her as if this were her professional job. But she doesn't
understand the restrictions beneath the waistline.

I never wanted to get married, he discloses.
Marriage should be a two- or three-year contract. Designed to be
renewed like apartments or cellphones.

So, it has been three years. What do you want to do. You want to
renew or go for another company? Switch carrier?

I don't have kids. As I was saying.

MAY I HAVE YOUR ATTENTION PLEASE

One beep.
Two beeps.
Three beeps.
May I Have Your Attention Please?
May I have Your Attention Please?
The light safety system is being tested.
This is only a test.
Please disregard all alarms until further notice.
May I Have Your Attention Please?
May I have Your Attention Please?
The light safety system is being tested.

This is only a test.

Please disregard all alarms until further notice.

One beep.

Two beeps.

Three beeps.

May I Have Your Attention Please?

May I have Your Attention Please?

The light safety system is being tested.

This is only a test.

Please disregard all alarms until further notice.

May I Have Your Attention Please?

May I have Your Attention Please?

The light safety system is being tested.

This is only a test.

Please disregard all alarms until further notice.

CALLOUSLY TOUCHED BY THIS MANIACAL MAN

David has been married to his wife, Imogene, for a long time. They celebrated their tenth anniversary just over a month ago. David is a banker. Managing clerks and money are his professional strengths. Outside of the business environment, David's most remarkable trait is his magnanimity toward his wife. David loves his wife dearly. Imogene, his wife, works as a consultant for a water softener firm. Sometimes she travels. Most of the time, she spends her day standing on the 44th floor in an office surrounded by glass, watching the second hand of the clock move a centimeter over and then another centimeter. Sometimes she thinks that time is glued to 3:20 pm. Imogene calls down to the help desk and demands that a mechanic come to her office immediately. The mechanic takes the elevator to her floor and informs her that the clock is not broken. It's just moving very slowly, as it should.

Some would say Imogene is restless and bored with her job. She is not bored with her marriage. As soon as the clock strikes five, Imogene is quick to dash out and return home to her husband who cooks her dinner and massages her feet. Which leg do you desire the most attention to? David asks, as soon as she enters the house. Imogene sprawls out on the sofa while her husband attends to her most intimate needs. Once in a while, he would suggest that she quit. She wouldn't have to stare at the clock and get angry purposelessly. He doesn't mind bringing home the dough. He means it. At the end of the year, for being the Banker of the Year, David earns a generous bonus. His subordinates ask, so David, are you using that huge perk as a down payment for a sports car? David smiles and says nothing. He has bigger plans for his extra earnings. While David mows the lawn, he begins to draw out a plan for how to please his wife most intimately.

As each day moves on and the seasons begin to change, David begins to notice that his wife is bored with practically everything. His massages, which he is husbandly known for, start to irritate her. Sometime in early Fall, she begins to treat his massages like hangnails. He would rub her feet, but she would immediately jerk away and crawl into a fetal position as if she were a ground-hog that had been found in a hibernating hole in the sofa. His elaborate gourmet display of icefish shattered on a tray of dried cream and dried horseradish root, and his elaborate assembly of roasted pistachio over goat's milk dipped in strawberry, is banal to her. She stares at his opulent display that took him an entire Saturday afternoon to perfect, and walks away as if he had served her proboscis worms. By winter, she has grown pale and short like snow. David begins to wonder what he might do to cheer her up. At work, he flips through a phone book and makes an appointment with a therapist. During lunch, he walks over to the therapist's office a few yard sticks away from the bank. The therapist tells him that it's possibly a seasonal thing. Moods fluctuate drastically during the winter months. Depression, she says, is just an expression of the mind trying to emulate the emotions and landscape of nature. Nature holds up a mirror and humans reflect. David assures the therapist that this is abnormal behavior for his wife. He tells her that he has spent ten winters with her and this is the first winter the glass has been clouded with sadness and there is no reflection. This is a lacuna. Something has changed in her drastically. He feels that if he doesn't do something about it, he may lose her. I don't want to lose my wife, David declares to the therapist feverishly. Realizing that she can't simply brush him off with general therapeutic advice, she considers further. A light arrives to her psychoanalytical head. She tells him that light boxes are great during the winter months as there is less sunlight. As soon as he gets home from work, instead of massaging his wife, he goes online and orders twenty light boxes from Amazon. He even clicks the button for express delivery. They will arrive tomorrow. Tomorrow, perhaps my wife's mood will change.

When the light boxes arrive the next day, he plugs every single one into every electrical socket available. The house is lit up like a museum. At five, the day is dark. When she enters the house, she screams. At first she thinks that her home has been converted into a science lab and that her husband is going to group five or six light boxes together, lay her body on them, and light her up as if to X-ray her. To see what body parts he can remove without killing her. To assuage her irrational fear, he unplugs them, stacks them, and stashes them in the deepest recess of the basement.

He returns to the therapist and tells her the result of following her advice. Bring her in, the therapist suggests. No matter what David does or how he tries to persuade his wife to see the therapist, Imogene refuses. She goes to work and comes home and nails her body to the sofa. Then there is nothing I can do for you, David. I'm sorry. If she doesn't come in, I can't treat her indirectly through you.

All winter Imogene enters the hole in the sofa and cries. When she gets off the sofa, David wonders if the dark pool of light on the sofa is Imogene's tears or the sweat. It's as if Imogene has managed to carve her shadow into the sofa. If David wishes to retrieve his wife fully from her dark state, he would also have to cut the sofa into a bowl and scoop the remainder of his wife's emotional baggage with him. David suffers a great deal during those long months. The winter drags on. Long hours sitting next to his wife on the sofa while she weeps and his heart aches. Sometimes he thinks that at the rate of her weeping, she might flood the sofa and he might have to get a raft and oars just so that they can sit on the cushions without getting wet.

Poor David.

To prevent a flood, every ten minutes or so he takes a few tissues from the Kleenex box on the table and wipes her tears. Then he folds the tissues into quarters and wipes his own. The winter moves on endlessly. When spring arrives, David's heart shows signs of some hope. Perhaps the pinkness of the cherry blossoms will color Imogene's cheeks and emotions. Spring arrives, but there is hardly any change in Imogene's mood.

Then one day, in the middle of spring, David gazes at the clock and at the door. At five thirty, his wife almost always barges in. Six o'clock arrives, but no Imogene. At first, David is mildly confused. Perhaps he had missed something in the early morning when he was running late for work. David roams the house searching for a piece of handwriting or a note. When he sees none, his heart grows heavy with restlessness. This is what my wife must feel every day at work, David thinks. This restlessness. These endless minutes and hours. David begins to think irrationally. Perhaps my wife has left me without letting me know. This is so unlike her, David reasons. But then her dark moods during the winter months were also unlike her. At seven, he calls the water softener firm. They inform him that his wife left at her usual time. Where could she be? Was she kidnapped? At eight, David tells himself, if she is not at the door, I will report her as a missing person to the police. When eight arrives, he calls the police. He can hear giggles in the background. Your wife is most likely not missing. It has only been two and a half hours. He informs David to report back if she doesn't come home the following day. David walks to and fro around his house, driving himself mad. He keeps glancing over at the kitchen table filled with stuffed eggplants and artichokes and pasta and desserts, dinner he had made for the two of them. Despite his wife's lack of appetite and weight loss, he continued to cook daily. Hoping that one of these days her appetite would return to normal. Not wanting things to spoil, he saran-wraps every plate and inserts them into the refrigerator. The refrigerator is packed with food. Certain gourmet dishes go as far back as November. David is oblivious to the smell.

Then he hears footsteps and then the front door cracks open. Imogene enters, her hands filled with shopping bags and a plastic sack containing leftovers from Olive Garden.

IMOGENE: Hello, David! Darling, would you help me carry this into the bedroom?

David bends down to collect her bags. Imogene's cheerfulness spikes up at an alarming rate.

DAVID: Where have you been?

IMOGENE: Didn't you get the message I left you at the bank? About going shopping with my girlfriends?

DAVID: When did you leave the message?

IMOGENE: Five minutes before I left work.

DAVID: I've been coming home fifteen minutes early from work because I wanted to be here for you.

IMOGENE: I'm sorry, darling. I didn't know.

DAVID: Well, I am glad you are in a better mood.

IMOGENE: It's the afterglow of shoe shopping. They have such great deals. I got these gorgeous red shoes for only $19. They were originally $150. Can you believe that?

DAVID: I can't imagine.

IMOGENE: Then we went out to eat. My gosh, I couldn't believe their key lime pie. David, it was just to die for. I didn't know I had such a voracious appetite.

DAVID: I am so happy that you are eating again!

IMOGENE: Oh, darling, I'm sorry. I know you've been in

the kitchen, slaving away. I promise to eat what you make
tomorrow.

DAVID: Alright, it's a date.

IMOGENE: It would have to be later though, you know. Like
eight or nine. The girls and I are hanging out again.

DAVID: We rarely eat dinner at eight. I'm all for newness.

IMOGENE: Well, I better head to bed. It's going to be crazy
tomorrow.

Imogene's mood escalates and escalates, as if her emotions were
hot-air balloons. David doesn't question it. If she is happy, thinks
David, there is no need to wonder if her balloons will come
down or if the explosive heat of the balloons will make her emotions stay afloat.

David begins to take her mood one day at a time. As long as she
is not weeping into the sofa, everything she does excites him. His
wife would come home with large shopping bags. Simple, floral
spring dresses and summer dresses in all sorts of styles. Then
radiant halters and swaying skirts and sleek shoes in all different
colors. Imogene is enigmatically cheerful. When Imogene shifts
from clothes and shoe shopping to perfume, David begins to
work overtime, even after the bank closes, to make more money
to feed his wife's new shopping habits. David does not utter a
single word of complaint. At the rate of her shopping, David
may have to convert the guest room into a closet space. As the
bills come in, David begins to pay them off systematically. He
begins to refinance their house, lowers their monthly mortgage
payment, and increases his payments on bills from thirty different retails stores. When Imogene begins jewelry shopping,
David takes on a second job working weekends as a construction
worker. He comes home on Saturday and Sunday with his hands

bleeding. His wife cheerfully clicks her heels back and forth. She spends long hours gazing in the mirror. Checking and rechecking the hem of her skirt. She dresses for work as if she were entering a pageant. She even goes as far as wearing a long evening gown, as if she were going to the prom. Her mood is high and she seems to take enormous pleasure in all aspects of life. Despite working longs hours and weekends, David too is content. Hearing his wife breathing next to him like an open fuse of sizzling gas instead of crying on the sofa, he is glad. He would breathe heavily from the long hours of work, but come home with his heart filled with contentment and joy. If he had known that working so many hours and shopping would bring his wife pleasure and him happiness, he would have done it a long time ago instead of waiting till now.

His wife lines rows of perfume bottles on the windowsills like transparent nutcrackers. He takes out his Banker of the Year bonus to pay them off as he is running out of time and weekends to add another part-time job. Originally he had stashed it away to get his wife a motorcycle for her birthday. She told him a long time ago that she had always wanted to lead a wild life; he'd thought immediately of a Harley-Davidson. But now he has run out of time to acquire additional jobs and her shopping lifestyle has grown wild.

One evening, he clocks out at the bank and returns home at nine o'clock to find his wife weeping into the sofa. Oh, no, David thinks. This cannot be. What's wrong? David asks. Imogene shakes her head back and forth. David pulls two tissues from the Kleenex box, dries his wife's eyes, and then folds them into quarters to wipe his own. They fall asleep on the sofa. The next day, David comes home at nine to find his wife on the phone, chatting away cheerfully with one of her girlfriends. David is relieved. But the following day, her face is embedded in the sofa. Imogene's mood swings left and right, up and down, and switches on and off like a light. Imogene's shopping sprees decrease drastically. One day, Imogene is emotionally high and the next day, she is low. Low like the fog when it crawls on the grass. When she gets low, she alters the atmosphere of the entire house. One moment the house is in a verdant state of spring, the next day it becomes wet fall, their emarginated leaves changing their colors. David feels absolutely helpless and hopeless. At night, in bed, watching his wife fall asleep, her hair fanning out like black light, he wonders what he can do. There's got to be a way, David reasons. We can't go on like this.

Then Imogene's shopping drops away completely. As a result of David continuing to work weekends and nights, their income increases drastically. David returns to paying a high mortgage and replenishes his Banker of the Year savings. He abandons his construction job and stops working overtime. Dropping those extra hours allows him to be there for his wife whose mood swings move up and down like a seesaw.

David begins to investigate his wife's condition. There must be a solution to her mood. There is always a solution. He asks around. Some suggest that his wife is bipolar and that he shouldn't try to be a doctor. Just admit her into a hospital, one of his collogues suggests. Another tells him that he has tried all he can, more than he can. He should just let her be. He confides in his best friend, Jackson, a philosopher. Jackson theorizes that his wife's behavior is a result of long-term nuptial conditions gone awry because they are childless. Children are a simple solution to boredom. When couples are childless, they manufacture crises that normally accompany raising a child (weeping randomly; lots of shoes and clothes shopping) and project them into a marriage. Jackson suggests that David shoot his procreative arrows into his wife's uterine walls and see if her condition changes. Jackson assures him that pregnancy has the ability to extract interior conditions and exhibit them externally. David nods and listens to his friend. Deep down, David knows that his wife's mood is not the result of lack of child rearing, but something else. Something he can't put his finger on. He will have to do the investigation on his own. The logics of his friends and colleagues are becoming more and more like tabloid columns. Eventually, during one lunch break, David walks into the main foyer of the water softener firm to speak with one of Imogene's colleagues. They inform him that other than the fact that she has been arriving to work wearing glamorous clothes and smelling like a perfume factory, there has been hardly any change in her. As he ascends the 44th floor, he flippantly asks the janitor about his wife. She surprises him. She discloses to him things her colleagues wouldn't, that his wife has been seen with a wild man, black leather pants, tight and super tight, she repeats, and he must have dumped her because one day she caught her crying while standing unmoving on this very elevator. David grows enormously sad because his wife is heartbroken. He hadn't known. How could he have known? He asks her if she knows what his name is. He asks fine details about his wife's lover. She discloses everything. He tips the janitor a hundred dollars. She refuses, but accepts it after he tells her that she has saved his marriage.

Every day during lunch, David drives over to his wife's workplace and observes his wife and her lover. He even gets binoculars. Some afternoons, David finds her arms linked with the man in tight black leather pants. She smiles brightly. Her eyes are luminescing like the sun. On days like these, David is so over-joyed that his heart tightens like ropes on lamb meat. On other days, the man in tight leather pants is standoffish and treats her like trash. On days like these, it breaks David's heart to see his wife being tossed around like a grocery sack. After several weeks of observation, David comes up with a solution. One day, after his wife returns to work and the man in tight pants gets on his Harley-Davidson and drives off, David follows him. He stops by a bar to drink a couple of beers with some people before hand-ing over a package. Then he drives back to his trailer home and plays video games while his wife slaves away and looks after five crying children, all under the age of ten. David follows this bad boy for a week before he completes his plan. As Imogene reen-ters her firm crying after a lunch break, the man in tight leather pants gets on his Harley-Davidson and drives off. David follows in tow. He tailgates him and jams his frontal bumper against bad boy's back tire. The man in tight leather pants flares up in a sudden rage. His expensive bike, blemish-free and gleaming black like a smooth panther, has been callously touched by this maniacal man. He swirls his bike to one side to let David's SUV pass him. As he passes him, the bad boy revs his engine, runs his bike parallel to David's driver side and roars, before swirling his bike as he plants it a few inches in front of David's front bumper. Almost losing control and swiping the bad boy's bike clean or knocking him over, David awkwardly pulls his SUV to the gravel side of the road before the vehicle bobs on the grass like the four hopping legs of a bunny rabbit. Wanting to give him a lesson in manners, the infuriated biker pulls over. Prepared to confront an idiot, David takes out a knife, turns around, walks up to the bike whose wheels have formed a cloud of dust around the grass and gravel, and holds the knife before the man in tight leather pants.

DAVID: You must be Stevie.

STEVIE: Fuck off. Who are you?

DAVID: Nobody.

Stevie tries to get back on his bike, but David overpowers him
and pushes him off.

DAVID: You know the water softener firm?

STEVIE: Yeah.

DAVID: There is a beautiful woman there you have been, what
is the word, courting.

STEVIE: I don't know what you're talking about.

DAVID: If I see her crying again, I am going to find you and
cut off your balls. You are going to treat her right.

STEVIE: I'll report you.

DAVID: I wouldn't do that. Life in federal prisons for selling
drugs isn't all that fun.

STEVIE: You have no proof.

DAVID: I don't make threats unless I'm armed.

STEVIE: You...her brother or something?

DAVID: See...this is how it is going to go. If she wants a ride
on your Harley-Davidson, you give her a ride. If she wants
a fancy date, you give a fancy date. If she wants a good
fuck, you give her a good fuck. The most important thing
is that she is well pleased. If she is crying, she isn't pleased.
She is suffering.

STEVIE: Well, she won't suffer. I'll just walk away.

DAVID: I wouldn't do that. It would make her suffer. She has
to call it quits on her own terms. So you go along with it
until she calls it quits. If she wants it for three years, you
give her a freaking three years. But if she cries, you won't be
around very long. Mark my words. You want me to carve

this message on your stomach in case you forget?

Stevie quivered, moving his head side to side.

> DAVID: If she dies or something happens to me, documents
> of your drug trafficking will be handed, as shown in my
> will, to the proper authorities. You will then squirm like a
> salamander who has misplaced its tail.

David walks back to his car, climbs in, and drives away.

His wife begins to transform in drastic ways. She comes home
bubbling with glee. Her happiness arrives consistently and regularly. She stops crying into her sofa. David smiles between bites
of his sautéed salmon and watches his wife's head toss in the sea
of light from the kitchen as she giggles her way into his gourmet
concoctions. Once in a while, he would accompany her to the
retail store and help her select a gorgeous dress for work. Once
in a while, he would surprise her with a pair of glistering earrings
that match her shoes. At night, when she falls deep into sleep,
he runs his hand along her curves. He kisses her naked neck and
exposed shoulder before falling asleep. David is so happy. He
pulls her tightly into his arms. Happiness is always within reach,
he thinks. He smiles before sinking into his subconscious.

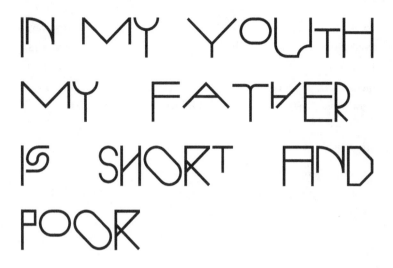

IN MY YOUTH MY FATHER IS SHORT AND POOR

I.

In his youth, my father is short and poor. En route to New York, the boats wear white shrouds as they float down the sea funeral. A sea so rich it fills the belly of my eyes with squid ink. From the base of my tongue, an image of my mother lifting me and giving me a wine bath made of dusty strawberries and red swollen grapes. In a hospital bed white like snow.

II.

I am on the phone with my brother while he asks a strawberry to pee. Pee, little strawberry. In the future the soul will be converted into a credit card. In order to make an emotional or intellectual transaction, the soul must slide the card into a slot inside the body, under the arm, near the bones of the right or left hand. Depending on the wealth of the soul, the card will have unlimited access to a storage space of instincts and intuitions and a warehouse of noetic supplies. It's depicted in cyberhistory month that King Solomon holds the highest credit score, though that data is questionable. Once in a while, an individual is able to purchase another person's memory or hair follicle.

III.

My body is pre-historic and you are waging war privately with the blowdryer, says the cauliflower as it is being shaken awake by beauty enhancement machines.

IV.

I hate to drive a porn star home from a bar. I hate it. I hate it.

ASHAN

Ashan wants to help everyone in the world because he has all the time in the world and he wants to make it a better place for someone or anyone. Yet, no one wants his help. At the grocery store, he tries to lift a basket for a young Asian woman and she stares at him as if he were a rapist. At the deli, he tries to remove the cart blocking pedestrian traffic so that two old men can get to the baguettes, but the men shout at him for trying to take their cart. Ashan doesn't understand why the world is so quick to misunderstand him. Outside, about to cross the street, he notices a small dog trying to eat some broken glasses and he walks over to shoo it away, but the fat owner berates him for being unkind to her canine and tells him very harshly not to talk to her dog that way. He droops his shoulders after crossing the street. He feels hurt all over and it is such a windy day. As always, the wind is so massive and invasive. When there are knives inside him, they leave slices of orifice in him, exposing his insides to air. His skin feels extremely sensitive. In the wind, there is nowhere to hide, especially in the open field. He couldn't even hide under the cypress trees because they are too tall and too skinny and there's not enough bulkiness to shelter him from the cruelty of the world. The world is a place where cruelty has all the swords. For each footstep he steps out into the world, a blade is plunged out and attacks him. At the bank, a blade hides between a fat patron and a skinny patron and out of nowhere that sharp object would assault him. With each attack he feels lonely and lonelier.

Some days, he stands in front of the kettle as it cools down and cries into it as the steam steams his face. Some days, the steam wears him like a mask and someday he would wear the steam as a mask. But this mask can't protect him from the coronavirus. What this mask is good at, is evaporation and condensation. This mask is a mask that should be worn when it's hibernally cold. A hibernal cold is a type of cold that can preserve its own visage and physiognomy. A type of cold that won't get uncold. Sometimes he weeps near the refrigerator and sometimes, if he is more sad than usual, he opens the freezer, digs his face into one of the freezer bins, and cries into it. His frozen tears are sometimes difficult to distinguish from the ice. He wishes there were a tear machine. It would cry for him on his behalf.

And, when others ask if he is capable of being sympathetic, Ashan would take out his ice-cubed tears from the freezer and drop them into a highball glass. He'd ask them if they could taste his sadness with their whiskey. They would nod their heads, but in fact, they are just nodding because his tears are too salty and make their tongues salivate too much to say anything. Once they finish swallowing, they realize that they don't have anything to say to him, so they just stare at his massive thumb and his tiny pinky. They study him hard, hoping that through their concentration they can make his thumb dumb and his pinky rosy as in salmon-pink, and that is the upper limit of their ability to understand the content of Ashan's hands.

He eventually walks home because no one wants his hugs or his help. He walks into the third floor of his apartment. He stops by the trash bin and asks it, Are you more sad than me? Or am I more sad than you? And, the trash bin is confused and refuses to answer. When Ashan enters his apartment, he sits down by the ottoman that looks like a dog and he tries to bark at the ottoman to see if it will leap over, hug and lick him. But, the ottoman is just a leg stretcher. It doesn't understand the language of affection or neediness. It doesn't know how to bark or sweep the floor with its ears and nostrils. All the ottoman can do is just sit and be a foot mat or a door mat if there is a door nearby.

When night falls, Ashan climbs into his bed and three large tears fall on each of his cheeks. He doesn't even wipe them away. He doesn't even walk towards his freezer to preserve them. He doesn't care if he is wasteful with his tears. He doesn't want to serve his guests his tears anymore in the form of ice cubes. He just wants to go back out in the world and help a prostitute with her job. Can I blow men for you? he asks. I am really good at it, he clarifies. But she shakes her head back and forth. She turns towards him, I don't want to be out of a job if they end up liking you. And so he wanders the streets in the dark, hiding his body behind an alley, weeping to the dark, forlorn, semen-smeared brick walls.

What should I do with myself? Everywhere I go, I am unwanted. I am not a needy person. I have just been self-quarantined in a world that has been self-quarantined for three decades, since the dawn of the internet. People tell him left and right to social distance himself and to wear masks not made of steam or ice and to use hand sanitizers, but all of his life he has been doing just that. And, now with everything under quarantine, he feels invigorated with despair and desperation. Sometimes he just wants to run out into the street and kiss a stranger. He doesn't care if he gets the virus. He doesn't care if his lungs collapse. He doesn't care if he dies. He has been so socially starved for so long and that starvation is a type of loneliness that makes him feel homeless and out of place. By now there are a thousand knives of loneliness and desolation in him. He could not even pull out a blade if he had the skill or mentality for it.

At 3 a.m., startled by insomnia, he walks to the kitchen sink and pulls out a real knife from a knife block. Not an abstract knife anymore, but a real one. And, he cuts his wrist with it. The pain runs out of him and when he gazes into the eye that is made from the slit, where the blood seeps out, he realizes that the eye is a door into the thousands of knives that have been stabbing his soul. He realizes that he is opening the door to something he will not know how to close and it's from this inability to close it that he discovers that blood is a type of loneliness too. But, this loneliness has a name and that name is suffering.

DIURNAL.

"I am beginning the walk at 11 am because the intense heat of the afternoon light has not become unbearable yet. Vegas is very direct about her scorchedness – & she is rarely shy about her blistering rage so if she is angry, you will know right away. First, I put on a wide brimmed hat, like a sombrero, to protect my face and my gloves to protect my hands. I am covered from head to toes. I don't even leave my ankle exposed. I learned this from my neighbor who had skin cancer in between his big toe and middle toe because it's a place in the body that one usually doesn't think to cover. I'm walking because I want to forget my body, my place in the world, and my sadness. It's a good way for me to unpack my dreams the night before. It's my way of having breakfast with my feet. I'm also walking because I love the desert, how dry the heat is, how it doesn't cling onto your skin, how the heat behaves like a cat, throwing itself at you by hurling itself off you. Now I'm out the door and I see cars whipping by, the casinos inside of the grocery store to my right. I walk slowly at first because the heat, in the early hours of its intensity, can be deceiving. Sometimes when I walk too fast in the heat, my body could become wobbly and I feel like I am losing consciousness, but I am not. Unlike some neighborhoods, a block of Vegas street seems very long. It seems like I am walking for an hour now even though it has been only a few minutes. I think the heat makes it feel longer. After walking one block, I stand still. I stand still for a minute or two. Then I study the tires on people's cars because I grew up in Long Khanh and have spent my youthful days just playing around rubber trees and these rubber trees would leak these latex odor and so I study these tires so I would feel at home in Long Khanh by being in Vegas. I take my sunglasses out from my windbreaker's pocket and put them on. Even though I am not looking straight into the sun, the brightness of Las Vegas makes me feel like I am staring straight into it. I notice a bright neon colored Mustang comes to a complete stop after flooring the car's pedal. Then the young boy from the passenger's window throws a McDonald's supersized soft drink cup near me. As it lands, it bursts the drink open, leaving the cup's strawed up lid twirling in a half circle on the hot pavement floor while the rest of it splashes itself near my legs. I ignore their intense roars of laughter and catcalling as I walk away from them. I walk with my tennis shoes half soaked in glucose. I ignore its stickiness by concentrating on Smith's fallen shopping cart which a shopper abandons near two or three short cacti and a pile of rocks after she loads her grocery into her apartment complex. I spend a minute or two staring at this shopping cart. I imagine pushing a handicapped rabbit in it as I walk. From pushing it, I could see the full view of its cottontail – how it twirls from the cart's vibration. The heat can change the garment of everything, including the garment of loneliness. Even if the desert is full of desolation, do you think the heat makes it less lonely? Do you think a very hot day can be an antidote to loneliness? Or is it its opposite?"

NOCTURNAL

"I am beginning the walk at 11pm because the scorching heat of the day is gone, and I walk away from the apartment in my flip-flops and without having to carry a bottle of water with me. I can feel my toes being ventilated, free to indulge in the Vegas calm, nonchilly air. Even though it's evening, it's still mildly hot. The heat doesn't have a breeze despite being so gentle in its intensity. I walk without a hat and I wear a short sleeve shirt. I now walk into Sin City without having to dress like a mummy, without being constricted by layers of garments and protective gear such as gloves and hat and long shirts, to protect myself from the sun. I walk fast because it's okay to walk fast without having to constantly hydrate myself. I sweat less during the night. I pick up my pace as the neutrality of Sin City's heat is gentle on my skin and pores. I walk with my back straight because during the day I have to hunch over a little when I walk to keep the sun from sneaking in beneath my hat to sunburn my cheeks. I can feel the full strength and wideness of my chest and my back as I walk. At the traffic light, I make eye contact with the driver who is about to turn left. I make eye contact because drivers usually don't expect to see a person walking in Vegas at a busy intersection at night and I don't want to be run over by a driver who isn't paying attention. After making eye contact, I cross the busy intersection. The intersection is a long walk because I need to cross five lanes in order to cross fully to the other side of the intersection. I make eye contacts with every driver I can make eye contact with. As I cross, I see my shadow being projected on the pavement created by their vehicles' bright headlights. My shadow grows bigger and bigger as their vehicles get closer to me before coming to a complete halt in front of me. My upper body jolts a little and I become startled a little each time they come to a complete stop because sometimes I think their brakes won't work and then I become one of those Iowa deer who indiscriminately cross the highway without looking left and right. Despite walking fast, and because the intersection is too long, and because I only make it halfway through the intersection, I stop and lean against the light pole between the crosswalk to rest. I stretch my legs using the light pole as a balance pole to balance my body against. I wait for the walking traffic sign to give me permission to walk again. I watch as the numbers decrease from 30 to 29 to 28, etc as I walk. I can hear the beating heartbeat of the walking street sign beating sonically as I walk. It always feels like another human, a human machine, is walking with me temporarily during this time. I walk past the bus stop where a man is sleeping on the pavement. He may be dead and I am afraid to touch him. So I dial the 911 number on my phone. An operator picks up and I tell her that there is a potentially dead man lying on the pavement near the bus stop. The operator tells me that they will send a police officer over. I tell them that it is the bus stop near the hospital on St. Rose. I end the phone call with the operator and continue to walk while my head stares back at the lifeless body of the dead man. I walk slowly and slowly until the lifeless body is only a small shrimp in the back of me. I walk and I walk until

I see the big red and white target sign of Target ahead of me. I know that I am getting closer to Krispy Kreme. My mother tells me that when their lights are turned on that means that freshly made donuts with their cream glazes are in the midst of being baked and fried and rolled out on the assembly belt and if I stop in, they will give one out for free. I keep my eyes for the lights but the Krispy Kreme bakery is more quiet than that dead man. Even if Krispy Kreme's light is on, I can't even try one on the spot because my body can't take gluten, but I like to wrap one in a napkin and walk with it in my hand home so I can give to my mother after she comes from her date with a businessman on OkCupid. I walk past Krispy Kreme and I walk and walk as the night is mostly silently. There are cars on the road, but they are whisking by me like they are traveling through time without any stop lights. I walk as far as I can and then I turn my body 180 degrees and walk back towards the bus stop that I have passed earlier. This time the Krispy Kreme's light is turned on. I walk in, ask the baker for one. While he retrieves a glazy donut for me, I watch the uniformed donuts being escorted through the assembly belt like they are nude ring-shaped life preservers entering the donut military. They march one by one down the line as they are being thickly coated with cream. He hands me the hot donut wrapped in waxed paper and I walk out of Krispy Kreme and walk and walk until I notice a homeless woman sleeping near a cement box next to a generator. Even though it is not cold, she sleeps with her body balled up, her legs tucked near her stomach. She looks like a piece of rock that can move and shift. She startles me with her existence. I watch her body elevate and fall from her breathing. She is alive and this time I do not need to pull my phone from my pocket to talk to another operator. I walk closer towards her and leave the Krispy Kreme donut near her body, next to the cement box, next to the dark green generator so that when she wakes up she can have something sweet to consume. Only on foot that she can be observed. I can see that vehicles driving by on high speed won't be able to see or notice her. Cars drive faster at night than during the day because they there is less traffic and less cars on the road. At the bus stop, I notice the dead man is being propped against the bus stop's metal seat. He is sleeping sitting up. He appears to be in a very uncomfortable position, and I regret calling 911 for him. If I didn't call, he would be sleeping more comfortably on the ground. At the light, I wait for the traffic light to say that I can cross the intersection. While I wait, I think: if one has to be homeless in a city, is Vegas the least ideal city for it? Or the most ideal?"

PART 3

THE MAN ON THE BUS KEPT FINDING REASONS TO TOUCH HER

The man on the bus kept finding reasons to touch her. First handling her bags, then shifting his position left and right and then touching her. He wanted to touch her because he needed intimacy badly. He kept telling her that his knees were aching and asking if she was a masseuse. She told him she was not. To follow up, he asked her instead if she knew of any masseuse. He sat there and, desiring tenderness, touched her. His fingers tiptoed across her skin like a child playing "I'll be quiet." But he was not quiet. His fingers were rustling like leaves. Fall hadn't begun. The summer broke out in heat. He smiled brightly at her, then inched his face further so that he could talk to another woman across her. A woman just landed on the seat next to her on the bus. She was curling her food-stamp application like a scroll, like Ancient China. He told her that she could have just filled out the form right there and submitted it immediately without having to return. He was trying to be helpful to the other woman so he could touch her. He asked her even if a woman were carrying heavy stuff, even if he was not his wife, he ought to give a hand. He began to scoot over to make room for other passengers getting on. No one sat down. He shook his head back and forth. He continued to talk to her about his knees. Yes, he used to live at that house over there. White house. Not the White House, but nonetheless the white house. He missed it badly. Three stories. The third floor was terrible on his knees. He moved and lived on the first floor now. Then he told her that he had ten siblings. Six sisters. He said he had nowhere to pee. One bathroom. His six sisters. They were in there putting on make-up. Crazy. He couldn't go to the bathroom. He kept on telling her. He was like a six-year old boy stuck in the body of a fifty-year-old man with bad knees and knew a lot about filing for food-stamps. It seemed as if everyone was eating off food-stamps. The old, the young, the healthy, the crippled, the deceased. He kept on talking and scrutinizing every passenger on board. He wanted to touch her so he touched her grocery bag. It would seem almost as if he were touching her. The grocery bag whistled a little. He smiled again. Another passenger got on. What time is it? he asked her. She told him. It sure took this bus long to get downtown. He kept inching his head lower and then higher like a pigeon. As if his head was trying to race itself. Here, here, here pigeon. I will race you. You get a head start. But the pigeon had a different idea. The pigeon just walked off to Wal-mart. He held his heart and gazed at the bus. The bus made a stop. The bus was switching drivers. The driver just dumped herself at a bus stop. A stop that was debilitating. It was an inhabitable bus stop. She got off; a man in blue uniform got on. He sat down and readjusted the seat, the mirror. He had to make adjustments while the man with bad knees kept trying to compete with the invisible pigeon who wouldn't play with him. He had six sisters and none of them wanted him to use the bathroom. She wondered about his bladder. He hadn't gotten off to pee. She believed he had a strong plumbing system. She wrote something on her iPod. He was increasing his excuse to touch her. If she kept busy, perhaps he would desire intimacy elsewhere. But his desire was focused. His desire was not ugly like the swimming suit bra the woman who had just hopped on the bus wore. She had scandalous skin. Skin six different shades of tan. Certain parts of her were peeling off. Not her clothes. But her skin and her hair were peeling and she wanted to sit down. She found a familiar passenger and sat on her lap. Everyone on the bus wanted to giggle. Back door, a voice hollered from the back. The bus driver had too much to do. He only remembered to open the front door. A woman carrying a portfolio got on. She talked about how her van was air-conditioned like this bus. She had nowhere to go, but to press herself sexually on the man climbing on the bus with her. He was wearing a tank top and khaki shorts. He tried to hold her together. Her face was sixty years old. His face was thirty. Her eyelashes were like a stroke of charcoal on the drawing pad of her face. But she didn't spray her face with an adhesive coat. She blemished. Eventually the passengers declined their seats by getting off at their stops. And the drawing pad woman and her boy toy sat down. They went over the details of her portfolio. A fat woman sat down with her blue lunch bag and when she sat down, she

VI KH NAO

occupied two seats. Another woman got on, exhausted, wanted
that second seat. Told the woman to scoot over. Expanding flesh
had no room, but she made room. She sat down between a man
and the fat woman as if she were a cork trying to force itself into
an opened wine bottle. She fitted, but she was high up. Dangling
between one fat and one muscular. The muscular man tried not
to breathe. When would the cork pop? He glanced around to
see if there were any sympathetic eyes. The bus pulled into the
downtown bus depot. Everyone got up quickly. Trying to be first
one out of the door. The man who had been trying to touch her
on and off offered to carry her bag, but she told him that she was
fine. Her knees were aching and there was a bruise on her thigh.
She wondered if his knee problems were contagious. This was the
last time he could touch her. He knew it and he grieved a little. A
little funeral sat next to him. The seat was gaudy and floral. His
knees were getting ready to burst open. He held on to his knees.
With his knee contraptions and his kneecaps. She got off the bus
and stared at the gleaming sun.

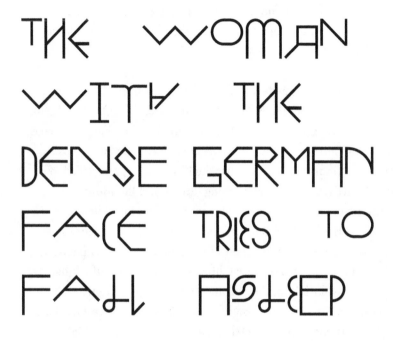

THE WOMAN WITH THE DENSE GERMAN FACE TRIES TO FALL ASLEEP

The Chinese woman asks about Providence. She is very Chinese and does not speak any English. Talk to my son. Is your bus heading to Providence? Clearly, of course. Thank you. Thank you. China has gotten on the bus and is heading to Providence. She is about to sit on a bag, but the man with the heavy laptop removes the bag so that China does not sit on his bag. There are twenty other empty seats. She takes one right next to him. At first, he hesitates to remove the bag. China does not understand cultural reference and appears aggressive. China is very lovely.

Her skin is almost white like a white woman. Her black hair is
jet black. She is a mother and because she is a mother, she is even
more lovely. Diagonally from her, the woman with the dense
German face tries to fall asleep.

The girl from the Hellenistic era sits across from China and
diagonally from the man with the heavy laptop. On the Megabus
chair, Helen looks like a plastic pump-able chair flattened green
before inflating. Helen is provocative. Helen is almost naked.
She gives the appearance that she just tosses a grocery sack out.
She arrives to the bus breathing heavily and flirtatiously smiles
to herself. As if arriving barely on time for a bus is heroic. She
tosses her hair back and crosses her legs. When she crosses her
legs, her dress lifts. It exposes the transparency of her panty. The
man can't see this because China is blocking him. If China were
to cock-block him, there would be a war. He can't grieve about
this because Paris, the son of King Priam and Queen Hecuba of
Troy, is not aware that Helen may have sex-induced thighs and
perceptible underwear.

Helen tosses her antiquated desire aside by stroking the table.
She is preparing and is making room for her arms which she
hasn't had a clue as what to do with yet. She strokes her hair after
stroking the table. She gazes far into the plexiglass landscape. She
strokes her own hair. The rain splatters. Behind her, umbrellas
are restraining their batlike, nocturnal membranous wings from
popping open. The umbrellas are coated with raindrops and a
familiar dank aroma.

The man types on his laptop. He can't gaze up. If he does, Greece
may pierce him with desire and later, sotto voce, declare him a
pervert. He strokes his keys. Social restraints have converted him

into an academic. Germany has been trying to fall asleep. She closes her eyes and blackens her eyelids with soporific canyons. Her eyelids are two knolls. Above the two knolls are hairy clouds. Later, one black cloud will fall off and land on her creamy cheek.

Germany gives herself a haircut of Cleopatra. Germany dozes in and out of eyelids. She snaps awake when a cellphone bursts into a jolly tune. She opens her eyes and glares. She glares at the mother and daughter sitting across from her. The mother laughs into the phone. Into the phone she mentions rain delay, traffic delay, and the impossibility of exiting New York.

New England is trying to stretch her legs out. Cars and buses climb onto her thighs. The rain is trying to knock the vehicles off her legs. The ambulances have disappeared into a crowd of rain. Helen removes her sweater. The mother turns to the daughter and states in a language that is not English that the sex-induced Helen is crazy. The mother has taken a dress and sport shirts recently purchased with price tags still attached and donned them on herself. She slips the dress around her shoulders and adds another layer of sport shirt made out of polyester. The rain and air conditioner are working too well. The mother sneezes.

Helen gazes out of the plexiglass windows and twirls her hair. It is impossible to imagine whom she is trying to seduce. One man who can hardly see her and four other women. Helen exudes no Sapphic odor or complications. Surely, she is seducing the air. Germany with her dense tone of Germanic implications decides to wake up and check her iPad. She flicks it open as if it were a mosquito that has aggravated her. She flips through the pages. She closes her iPad and dozes back into sleep. She does not smile when she enters the black wall of subconsciousness. The mother turns to the daughter. Her necklace is grotesque. It is going to sag her neck to the floor.

The daughter smiles. Is there any French in her? asks the mother. The daughter replies, she may have Norway in her, the texture of her skin, the color of her hair, but she is densely German. Oh, so true, states the mother. Her density is making her face hard. She has a hard face. Her hard face won't let her smile, says the daughter. The mother closes her phone, closes her eyes, and falls asleep. Helen gazes seductively at the daughter and twirls her hair.

Helen shifts her gaze, and then she smiles naughtily. Helen is awaiting the Trojan horse. While she waits, she seduces all the women nodding off to sleep. Helen is harboring naughty thoughts and Helen is not afraid. The world is going to sleep without Helen. Helen gazes past the plexiglass. The plexiglass is losing its plasticness through the dark light and is becoming glassier. Helen turns her face away from her reflection. Why seek glassy Narcissus when her flesh is her own lake? She strokes her hair and then she shifts it to her skin. She smiles to herself and exhales.

The daughter is afraid to breathe. She turns her head toward the driver. There is a screen above the driver's head. It is recording the faces of the passengers on the upper deck of the bus. If the driver gazes up, he can see who is soggy enough to fall over, to slant into the body of another passenger. The driver does not look up. The driver, the windshield wiper, and the night are fighting a violent war with rain. Rain continues to descend. The sloshing sounds of the wheels echo on the asphalt. No one is at fault. The night is ready.

The mother wakes up. She talks to a man on the other line and laughs. The bus is quiet now despite the rain. When the mother laughs, the silence of the bus gives the illusion that her voice is glowing in the dark. Flashes of green and red, neon and shaded, echo from one panel of glass to another. The bus is slowly becoming a woman. Throat gargled with sleepers and hips widened because of the rain. The bus is wearing shoes and is treading through mud. The mother closes her eyes after closing her conversation with the man. The density of Cleopatra increases as she falls deeper into her dream. Her face is angular like a sheet of paper. If everyone dies on the bus, the dreams will naturally stop falling away. Helen's sex-inducing thighs will be tossed around an ice bucket made of flesh.

The daughter asks the mother as soon as she opens her eyes. Which is safer? The upper deck or the lower? The lower, replies the mother. The mother's eyes fall back into her face. The daughter is wide awake. Helen turns to her and tosses her a gaze. Germany closes her eyes completely. Helen is interested in Paris, but Paris hasn't arrived with the Trojan horse yet. Helen turns to birth control devices:::::::women::::::for priapic fulfillment. The daughter removes her shoes from beneath the table and allows her wet socks to dry.

Helen strokes her hair. The bus battles rain. The bus hums like a woman. Traveling on the bus reminds the mother of dice being tossed down a casino table. When the dice land, the grass is always mowed, and the table is always green. Hands gather their belongings and take back what belongs to them. Traveling is a gamble. Empty handed, the passengers spent money and feel their intestines being dumped out onto the street. The night is dark while vehicles collect their bodies and throw them up three flights of stairs into a room made for humans and not animals. A deer walks out of a room and asks for laundry coins. Flashlight can only be described as electric lamp. The headlights of the bus are being massaged by the rain. Helen's mouth is smiling. Germany is stern. Germany has never been able to smile with eyes open or closed. America taps on his laptop. China is falling asleep. Her white face is radiating with shadows. China is smiling. Helen strokes her hair. China has no one to state her opinion about Helen. China is a mother and she is not easily seduced by other foreign countries, especially Greece. Greece is stroking the table now. China is ignoring Helen. Helen's body is faceless to China. Helen has beautiful, lustrous skin.

Birth control devices can't return erotic gazes. Birth control devices do not possess such feelings. The bus has not been able to fall asleep because the driver's eyes are wide open like a movie theater. Rain splatters. Greece strokes her own skin. A woman behind the daughter falls into the mouth of sleep. Germany wakes up and takes a bag of chips from her bag and chews. Germany's strong cheekbones are vibrant. The internal clocks of the passengers are shifting far right. America closes his laptop. Helen is on fire with desire and plexiglass is absorbing her hankering. When desire is facing glass and shadow, an echo of darkness crawls back into the pores of the skin. Helen's desire is crawling on its belly. No one is asking Greece to wear a wool coat. Panels of black light fall onto the bus. The driver is defenseless against Connecticut.

In the dark, even light is falling. The bus has no time to catch its breath until the driver stops and the driver switches. Beneath the tunnel, the bus breathes. No one gets off except the driver. A man walks on. The driver has taken his suitcase down. He

gets into a car. The bus driver waves. Later, Helen knows that
condoms will enter a condominium with her. Helen is aware of
this as her hand brushes past her breasts. She can't tell beneath
her grocery sack if her nipples are delighted with goosebumps.
Sometimes it's hard to get pleasure to crawl a certain way. Helen
knows this better than anyone. Germany wakes up and bobbles
her legs up and down so that her shoes are corks floating on a
cup of borderless air. Her shoes are perforated. Her calves are
heavy and she stops bobbling. Her necklace is ugly; her face is
stern. Density of Germanic heritage, Cleopatra ignores everyone.
Helen should kiss Germany to wake her up. Helen has a violent
tongue and has the ability to break the density, Berlin Walls of
teeth.

Helen strokes her hair and gazes past the plexiglass. If Helen were
a television show, her body won't stop strobing. When Helen
exits the bus, her bat-umbrella isn't afraid to bounce out and
navigate out from the cave of reality. Sound doesn't travel as fast
as light. Bat's eyesight is slower than human. Helen knows this as
she strokes the thighs of her Batman who greets her at the mouth
of the bus depot. Germany is quick to exit. In a flash, she is stern
and then she is gone. Insomnia remains on the seat, afraid to run
after Jewish air. It's hard to understand Hitler on a night like this.
Especially when Helen won't occupy Germany. Greece sneaks
away to Batman, America remains in his seat until China decides
to exit. The mother and daughter are the last ones to leave the
bus because the black photographs lying beneath a panel of
blue plastic decide to fall asleep and tuck themselves behind the
railing. It takes the daughter awhile to notice the discrepancy in
the chronology of belongings. The mother and daughter fly out
of the bus and dash after a yellow taxi. When the mother enters
the apartment, she is making oatmeal using fresh apricot that she

has sliced into thin panels of pink light. Germany won't remember the mother and daughter ascending a flight of stairs. America
is so tall. When he gets up, the ceiling of bus flattens his hair.
America is expected to be bald. Greece is spreading wide open
like a bat's echo. The headlights of the bus are a type of electric
kerosene. The bus driver doesn't have a urinary tract infection,
but does it matter if he urinates when it rains? In the dark, no
one is able to tell the difference between a penis and a potato
peeler.

CALM, CALM, CALM, RUPTURE

She has been eating tiramisu for 678 days straight and her thighs have expanded to a storage space. As she lifts her finger for the 679th piece, she reconsiders the origin of the word tiramisu. Its etymological root suggests that the sponge cake macerated in coffee and liqueur and mascarpone is extracted fully from the Italian phrase *tira mi sù* 'pick me up.' At the rate she is expanding, she wonders how anyone can pick her up. It dawns on her that perhaps the pick-me-up moment isn't referring to her, but to the cake itself. She begins to think about how she is an unreliable narrator to her very own hips. After all, if tiramisu and her hips can switch roles as protagonists, when her hips are snowballing, it's really the tiramisu that is truly enlarging.

She is dragging her body through the woods now, as there are no other ways to develop her infatuation for a danseur named Butternut. Butternut rehearses his steps and fluid gestures in the woods. His thighs move like scissors through different corridors of the wilderness cutting up leaves, fibrous forms of the branches, ferns, valleys of the lilies, trees, shrubs, black locust, sassafras, and when his steps halt in mid-pause on their way to her face, she becomes increasingly startled. At the rate he is moving, it does not surprise her if she does want a haircut badly, his feet would eagerly lift their blades and trim her bangs so swiftly that she'd end up looking marvelous, a voluminous replica of Cleopatra. She does not want a lavish cut. She wants only to lean forward and plant a kiss on him. As she leans in to him to do so, the gravity of her mass dilates and shifts the energy of the vertigo, and it makes him lose his balance. Inadvertently he kicks her nose, breaking it into seven even parts. Her nose looks like the spine of a stegosaurus. Her love, unlike her nose, does not become extinct and she grows exponentially in love with Butternut.

WHAT I STARVED BEFORE TURNING YOU INTO BLUE

I starved my head off, waiting for a decade to turn her body over. At last, the decade has arrived. Starving every centimeter of me— moving away from her toward the decade. Azul Eyes assure me that I am not a dress, as I suppress her breath behind fluttering doors. But despite not expecting her to be a pail of Spring, light and air surrender their hands over to me. Ropes climb the wall of the well. I haven't pretended to be panthers. I haven't pretended to be pantyhose. I haven't pretended to be anything as I compress every inch of spring into the earth. Every spring her mouth falls on my lap.

I met a French woman there. Perhaps an un-sexy version of Catherine Deneuve. But still very beautiful. I had broken a bottle of expensive wine at a Chinese restaurant while ordering Chicken Lo Mein. In Spain, there were no curtains of noodles.

The unfamiliar woman exclaimed in English, What a shame!
She nodded me over. Do you speak English?
I say I do not know how to speak French.
I have wonderful wine bottles at home. Don't feel too bad. I will give one of them to you. (Snobbish French? There is no such thing!, I thought)
Oh, no. That's very kind of you but I don't believe that is necessary.
I have a boyfriend in the states. I visit him once a year in Florida.
Would you like to have some tea at my home?

I turned my face to a flowerbed, wanting to say *No thank you* to earlobes that couldn't bend.

We walked out into the evening. Perhaps six o'clock in October. The streets were paved with people walking to and fro. Dirty pigeons hopped here and there. There was dog shit everywhere. At a supermarket, the lighthouse of the world, she helped me select a wine. She asked the clerk to find me a carton with handles. She talked deliciously and I wanted to throw cinnamon over her purse.

The stranger bought two tickets and we got on the night metro. I recalled the lights flickering on and off as we entered one tunnel and out into another. I enjoyed the way florescent light moved in and out of her face like a flashlight before a toilet seat and the way her white scarf was draped around her neck. She was French.

As soon as we got off, she, Nicole, wrapped her arms around me. We walked up a flight of stairs out of the metro. We were on Ulysses. Her home was on Ulysses. I walked a dark flight of stairs. And took the elevator up to 4th floor. She turned the keys and we were inside. She was a book lover. Her living room was walled and stocked with books that stretched forever from one corner to the next like a maze. I followed her into her hall-size kitchen as she turned on the gas stove. She poured water into the teapot. She turned back into the living room, spreading curtains open. It had gotten dark so suddenly. Tall and short edifices paved a path like a graveyard. At the center of this cemetery was the Eiffel Tower, standing like a pulsating heart. On the windowsill sat a little kumquat tree housing twenty orange balls. The wind fluttered over her little plants. The pot hissed violently. She walked back to the stove and I followed her.

She opened the lid of the pot. Holding a tight knitted strainer on top of the top, she shook the tea into the metal net.

I am opening the buds of the tea to extract its flavor. If I plunge the tea too quickly into the boiling water, it won't open as much.

Nicole was teaching me how to make love to a woman.

She poured me a cup and then a cup for herself. We walked to her bookshelves. This is my angel of love. My lover of ten years. He passed away three years ago. He is an angel. My angel.

There was a glass of snow stuck in her voice.
In French, angel sounded beautiful.
She showed me her nude paintings and told me that she had artworks in galleries around town.

She asked me where my angel was.

I said, She is on her way to coming into the world.
I told her about the Asian woman I had fallen in love when I was fifteen. I told her that it had been nearly four years and she still doesn't know.

Asian's love is a bit slanted. Eastern culture loves with their eyes. Western with their cunts. You should make love to her when you get home. No, no. Not figuratively, literally.

Nicole, she is taken, I informed.

You should make love to her anyway. You'll find out immediately if you should spend your heart that way. She'll thank you for it. Your heart, too.

Don't tell her how you feel. It will turn out very badly. Make love to her. Make her tea. The body speaks a language that the mind will never comprehend. Learn that language. When the body doesn't like the taste of what it's consuming, the mind changes flavor. The East doesn't like to consummate. The West loves to. May I escort you to the museums tomorrow?

My bus departs at 7 am.
If you ever come back to France, call me or write me. I want to show you around.

For three hours we spoke intensely and intimately. I left her place and returned to my hostel still infused in the aroma of tea, the scene of the Eiffel Tower, the kumquat tree, her glorious books, her nude artwork, her address. On the way back to Granada, her conversation replayed itself in my mind.

When I got into the states, I took the lotus route into deformity. What an odd woman, to hand her mouth and eyes over to me.

VIGNETTES: EXPLORATION OF CERTAINTY & UNCERTAINTY

VIGNETTE #1:

There is a history of men carrying Adela across the bridges. At the end of the bridge, they lower her down to the ground next to a ginkgo tree. She inhales the tree's pungent aroma and sits down beneath it. Adela is aware that her death is waiting for her across the river. Where is the bridge? Where is the long corridor? After death, there's only white light: incorruptible and indisputable.

VIGNETTE #2:

Adela and her mother spend every single moment with each other. They eat breakfast together; they tend to the garden together; they pick apples at a nearby orchard together. They sit in the parlor eating French bread, sipping tea, and even reading the same book. Like twins, Adela and her mother are inseparable. And then one day, they have to be separated. Their organs recede back into their original cells. Their eyes grow so small that their eyeballs fall off the waistlines of their sockets. They sink into their brain. Their fingers become smaller. Their eyelids wilt. They wonder why on earth God puts them into one crate and later sends them asunder like eggs into the world. They hop from one nomadic basket to another. Then one day, while walking her daughter home, Adela notices a metallic, watery pool undulating on the surface of the asphalt. Her mother's blacken yolk is speaking to her.

> MOTHER: I haven't been able to deliver into our bodies the things we want.
> ADELA: I will give you, Mother, a copy of my stillborn.
> MOTHER: Does the poetry translator carry a photograph of the poet he translates?
> ADELA: So, Mother, do we hold back our tongues?
> MOTHER: Because your father and I couldn't penetrate that way. With each other. Let's analyze the stars with our spine. Your father's tongue moved up & down my body like the double helix. When your father made love to me, your father & I are just one thumbtack amongst millions of other thumbtacks, pinning the skin of the earth in place.
> ADELA: We want poetry that doesn't go far.
> MOTHER: You are wide open, child, to receive everything that comes before you. You who open your hands and legs. You who have mouths that eat intensity from skin. I believe you don't have any fleece on you. Your face extends out on my face.
> ADELA: How far and how wide is your understanding of the

sun. How much will your body go? Rosy like a scarf dangling off your body.

MOTHER: Who is fighting for longevity?

Adela's mother murmurs the night into Adela's skin. Her
mother is reduced and exposed to black light.

VIGNETTE #3:

Vince is afraid of his wife. He is afraid of his wife's infidelity.
Each morning before she descends the stairs, he measures the
length of her skirt from the floor and the dimensions of her back.
He measures her this way as to prevent her from thinking that
she can expand that way, expand in a way that she can only expand when she is outside of their home. Vince is also convinced
that happy people tend to get chubby and round. If his wife is in
love with someone else, it's only natural that she becomes robust
and spherical as possible. When he measures her, it's a reminder
to her and to himself that her waistline can only go so far. But
how far is so far?

VIGNETTE #4:

The room remembers to recombine. How far wide and how far
wider is it to expect a dream to follow a life? How is it possible to
move a mountain without expectation? The forehead is removed
into a room, closing the doors and minds. Words displace themselves on the page. The birds are chirping, waiting to surrender
their monstrosity in a heartbeat. After the windows move around
the house, the windows become widows of a house, husbandless

from eating light. That is what windows do. They come right into a house and ascend the siding and then bask their mouth in the moving sun and inhale light. And when they eat light as much as they do and sometimes air, they remember their life before they were glass and metal and wood frames—then they eat light.

VIGNETTE #5:

This vector is beautiful. Adela hasn't been able to deliver into her bodies the things they want. So they hold back their tongues. Adela has time to sacrifice her lungs. Tongue switching. Moving along the water. Her face resurfaces and her lungs expand. The voice of Adela—
I stand here gazing at the piano as I cannot spread apart nor turn my face away. If I were not at my own philosophy course, I would depart from myself and watch a piano recital. I would not turn back to look at me. I would go on as if nothing destroyed me. It is because I am incredibly small that I stand before myself alone.

VIGNETTE #6:
Snail & Widowers—
Are you going to pry me open with a crowbar?

VIGNETTE #7:

Adela dreams that she is a shepherd of women. She gathers

100,000 of them. She cuts open each of the woman's stomach lining and uses their alimentary canals to make one boat. Will the boat sink or will it float? Adela wonders why her dream is making a boat. Aren't memories vain? Easily flattered by the scent of scent and scent of light?

SHE IS NO LONGER ON VACATION WITH A HOLE

She has been away from the structure of things. Clasping her thigh. Some sentences move other sentences without knowing. She has known her legs could do this; prevent the sun from coming to her in a certain way. Stroke of darkness. She overhears everything. Does she remember how the sentences are stroking on her? Cream on the sun. Sunscreen screaming at the sun. She is no longer on vacation with a hole. The sun is glancing behind the cloud. Sometimes the wife thinks the sun is a grown up man with a burning sensation to lose it all. After that, the sand comes around. Twirling with the pink mini-shovels. Behind the umbrella stand, a orange bucket is confronting the lifeguard. Clearly, someone has to die. The children keep on dipping their hands into the sand. Arenose hands. The wind will blow the sand off their hands. The mother is walking slowly towards herself. She will never make it. The sun's desire has cast the shadow around the hip on the ground. He won't move. The husband. He is sprawled out on the neon beach towel as if he has drowned. His wife asks him to move aside. Her shortened self is rocking his face back and forth. There is a large breeze and she is wearing a shirt-skirt. She won't discriminate against him for not wearing a hat. But he should wear a hat.

WIFE: Why won't you wear the hat I gave you for your birth-day?

HUSBAND: I left it at home. It would blow away.

WIFE: You could put a rock on it, or that orange bucket over there.

HUSBAND: It's hard to wear the hat with that on top of my head.

WIFE: The bucket is meant in case you don't wish for it to blow away.

HUSBAND: This is why I don't wear it. I don't want it to blow away.

WIFE: I shouldn't have given you a hat.

HUSBAND: I'm glad you got me a hat. I don't have any.

WIFE: You don't wear it.

HUSBAND: I can't wear it. It would blow away.

WIFE: Sometimes you just have to take chances.

HUSBAND: Not on a windy day like this.

WIFE: It's sunny, for godsake!

HUSBAND: It's both sunny and windy.

WIFE: I shouldn't have gotten you that hat.

HUSBAND: The hat isn't even here.

WIFE: Because it isn't here, I see it everywhere. It's the oppo-site of having a husband. You know. He is everywhere, but you don't see him.

HUSBAND: I am right here, darling.

WIFE: Exactly my point.

HUSBAND: Your shadow looks so odd from this angle.

WIFE: Really?

HUSBAND: Your shadow looks so shortened.

WIFE: It's rocking across your face.

HUSBAND: My face?

WIFE: My shadow is rocking across your face.

HUSBAND: Then, stand still.

When will the farm farm the body? This is the question that the wife never asks the husband on a beach day. It is a beach day for them both. They work long hours at a factory making oatmeal all day. The entire city smells like oatmeal. Their skin smells like oatmeal. They eat only cereal. No one has stopped them from doing so. They continue to boycott oatmeal secretly in their own homes. History neglects to record silent boycott. History doesn't want to be responsible for being unaccountable. No one makes historians accountable. The husband scoots aside to make room for his son's approaching scooter. His son carries it tucked beneath his armpit as he approaches. The scooter is useless on sand and thus the son is in a terrible mood. He approaches his mother and father as his mother lies down on the beach towel next to the husband. She is afraid to get sand on the beach towel so her legs are angled in the air as if she were a chair that had just reclined. The son's shadow is speaking to them, but it's hard to distinguish where the lips are exactly. To look up is to be burned away by the son. The moving lips of the son. But the mother and father gaze up.

SON: When can we leave?

HUSBAND: We just got here.

SON: When can we leave? I'm bored out of my mind.

HUSBAND: Ask your mother.

SON: Mom, when—

WIFE: No.

SON: Mom, said 'No.'

HUSBAND: I can hear that.

WIFE: Your father is everywhere. I mean everywhere.

SON: Dad, can't you convince mom that we should go?

HUSBAND: Why don't you convince her?

SON: I don't want to. She doesn't budge.

HUSBAND: Sure she does.

SON: No, she doesn't.

HUSBAND: I think they just opened up that new outlet mall
near the freeway. Do you want to see what is on sale there?
Do you think all the sale items are gone by now?

WIFE: Outlet mall? Really? Why am I the last to know?

HUSBAND: Let's definitely check it out.

WIFE: Let's go!

The wife gets up at the speed of lightning. In fact, she is in the
perfect position to do so. She just needs to be tilted over. She
does this by rocking back and forth. She does this without rocking back and forth on the husband's face. Her shadow does not
know how to cast itself over the sand when she is lying down.
She is up and about, moving with great zeal and verve. She lifts
the orange bucket up. The bucket doesn't want to be touched,
but now is touched and is being moved around like a baby.

SON: Dad, what have you done?

HUSBAND: I thought you wanted to get away.

SON: The mall is worse than this. She might be there for

hours! Even days if they permit it. And they don't let scoot-
ers in the mall!

HUSBAND: Why not?

SON: They don't want to be sued if I slip and fall.

HUSBAND: Well, if you don't want to go, you ought to talk
to your mother.

Mother is rushing back and forth trying to collect things into
their beach bag. Flip flops, sunscreen, magazines, etc.

SON: Mom, can't we stay?

WIFE: No.

SON: Man, I shouldn't have spoken up.

The son thinks, Mom, if you keep on behaving this way, you
are going to turn me into a monster. Mom's reaction to things
is like dropping a drop of water onto a mirror. Mothers are
relentless about shopping. Soon the umbrella is quite a distance
from them. They collect themselves and remove their weight off
the sand. The wife is quick on her feet and the son is dragging.
The husband is equidistant between the son and wife. He is the
lawyer everyone should get, but doesn't want. He is trying to
tie them together with legs and arms and shadows, but his wife
is moving very fast. If everything goes on sale, he is in a lot of
trouble. They have already refinanced the house. He isn't ready
to refinance their car. To please his son, he may have to sell their
house. His wife has clothes that still have the price tags on! And
they were not bought cheaply either. What will she do with the
newly accumulated clothes? Once she has her mind set on shopping, there is no convincing her out of it. The son knows this.
This is why his legs have turned to iron. She had been rocking his
face without him knowing this. He didn't even feel an ounce of

pleasure. Now, they are not relaxing at the beach. Instead, he will be holding large shopping bags for her, dragging his feet from one retail store to the next. And he will yawn. The ideal weekend turns into a nightmare. His son is going to hate him for this and he is going to hate himself for this. Surely, something can be done to change her mind about shopping. He can't buy her a diamond ring out of this. His wife has already shuffled everything into the trunk. She is leaning against the car door, waiting for them to arrive. Finally, they all make it to the car. Her shadow has already morphed into a pool of unsteady sweat and it is sitting next to her feet like a loyal, watchful puppy. Son glances at father, pleading. It's hard to tell who is pleading more. The hat of forgotten clumsiness. The upcoming tides of monsoon.

THE FORK IS BUSY SPOONING THE SPAGHETTI

Where can the chicken relive its memory? Along the inner seam
of its pluck-able skin. Yes, the chicken recalls: I am a bystander
to a suicide. I blame it on muscular dystrophy. The answer is
closely related to a farce that a face can't emulate. Run the pocket
home. Away from the ardor. Away from this inseam. Pocket the
charcoal block: lifetime retirement plan for suicide. A good way
to expunge the stomach from its pills of insincerity. Can't be
there. Won't be there. For the suicide. Soon enough, the stomach
is pumped up for the proper retirement plan. Charcoal won't
tolerate the treatment of purging. Evidently clueless about the
material of nakedness, naked wisdom. So they ran to face the
long face. They captured a particular kind of light, along the

edge of the mouth. Along that broken edge, insincere movement across the borders. Sometimes, cremation is important for the intellectuals, creaming the tomatoes, sit tightly together, compacted for the mouth. Ready, the dipping sauce hovers over the intellectual plates that will not intellectualize. So the men speak. So often. So not so often. Often yet enough. The forks intellectualizing the spoon. The fork is busy spooning the spaghetti, waiting for the men to abuse the absurdity of a conversation. They are, after all, in a meeting. Relentless, the dating game of Italian gourmet food. The men don't even bother to rotate. The pepper grinder. Won't improperly abduct the salt like a rooster, to hang it upside down and shake the salt out. It's over. The conversation, not the dinner. Mouths chew other people, thoughts across the table. They are fearless about their ritual of mastication. They are more fearful about the duck confit that isn't fitting into their fitting room. Much later in the evening, of course. There is not fitting room at a restaurant for business men and women. Before entering a window shop. If you enter a store, you defeat the purpose of window shop. You defeat a silent parade of can't have what you can't have. So of course, they asked the food to be packed to go even though their hotels don't have refrigerators. The men think they can stop wastefulness by elongating the decomposition process. I can't waste if I am saving for later. Of course, rotting is a perfect retirement plan for the pumped stomach of two men at a hotel room. Can't fuck each other. Not interested. So charcoal is the perfect date rape of the stomach. An accumulation of dying without dying. Pumping is majestic. It's impossible to please dinner, the chicken legs, AND the pepper grinder. It's not possible. Absolutely not possible. To die before a majestic queen size bed with two fluffy pillows. Cremation is the ability to sleep inside of a pillow by returning to powder. No one knows the secret of being tossed in the air into debris of sea and

ennui. Cremation isn't for everyone. If one eats creamy Italian
food before being cremated, does one's dust become creamier?
It, too, has powder. The result of proper treatment of luxury and
opulent appetite. Something has to make the canister beautiful.
It will just sit there. Can't taste itself. It can't lick itself. Everything has to happen all at once. Expunge, expunge, a chorus of
doctors circle around a mouth. The intellectuals like to eat parmesan cheese. The nurse is taking as many notes as possible. She
is considering this kind of date rape. She knows it belongs to the
intellectuals, but sure why not, for her too, if she tries. Things
not to do, she writes. Don't eat parmesan cheese, even if you like
it a lot. The doctors will smell and they will overanalyze. Stick
with chicken thighs. Slap the chicken thighs first before drowning down the chicken and the pills. Slapping guarantees muscular dystrophy. It won't walk away. It guarantees this. This is to
show also that retirement and cream aren't for everyone. No one
likes muscular dystrophy before being cremated, especially chick-
en thighs. Before attempting to die, the table is sitting next to
another table that had four women clamoring. They were smiling
like they had spent too much money on those Venetian shoes.
They held their breath across the table. The intellectuals thought
no one ever makes drawstrings for shoes. Women shoes. Drawstrings hide ankles and varicose vein. It's too late now to talk
the company into implementing drawstring for women shoes.
They will attempt to die together. Aging is applied to design of
women shoes, in this case. When they open their hotel doors,
they acknowledge that muscular dystrophy is for lonely people.
Of course, no one is capable of buying into the future. There are
homes in straight blocks that guarantee proper retirement and
quarantinization of elderly XY chromosomes. Of course, they
don't want to go home to be shuffled away. The doctors pump
their stomach. But it's not a well. It's not like a well at all. No one

can pass the bucket around to quench the thirst of others. No one dares. Why Italian food when it has so much carbohydrate? Why? & cream is so heavy before dying. Carbohydrate makes the soul sink deeper into purgatorial delirium. Lettuce is good consumption for suicide. It has to be. It is light and airy and crispy, not like sorrow in the carbohydrate spaghetti. When the fork is spooning, it wasn't thinking of the bow-tie noodle. Its triptych heart is 100% devoted to the spaghetti noodle. Long strings that made the intellectuals think of drawstrings for shoes. The women across the table. The intellectuals stop believing in their dinner. Why did they come here on the company's tab? Was it worth it? $100 dollars for a meal they didn't have to pay. They don't have anything to look forward to after the silence exits their stomach lining. They probably should have thought about the gun. Why didn't God invent drawstrings for the stomach? To isolate the pills from the carbohydrate. To tug and pull. To prevent other things from coming in especially when one is full of suicidal desires. No one is going to stop them now especially after the gorgeous view of Vegas. Sprawled out like an electrocuted octopus. When the ambulance came, the glass door has to be shattered. This is to say: it's hard to die silently. Even window breaks open because carbohydrate and pills and drawstrings are glamorous. The women were waiting for the inner thighs of chicken to cook a meal for them. So they waited for the chefs. The chefs delivered their food: the halibut wearing a drawstring dress made out of lasagna and spaghetti noodle. After that, their suicidal execution is unwavering. Before taking the pills, the men wrote to their dead wives in envelopes, curtesy of the hotel. They wrote: Please wear drawstring slacks when you greet me. I would like to think that if I spill something in you, you would be able to close it up. Here, on earth, if you spill, everything gets exposed.

HER UNDERWEAR, POMPEII

In front of a class of over twenty classmates, Elena must deliver her oral exam on Abraham Lincoln on Thursday, which is just barely two days away. Elena is anxious and worried. Her social studies teacher, Mr. Irvine, recommends that she practice her speech in front of a mirror. She thinks this is narcissistic and stupid, but she doesn't tell him that. Her parents, however, have a more promising suggestion.

"Elena," they begin. "Imagine that you are addressing a roomful of naked people."

She imagines Abraham Lincoln naked. His white thighs extraordinarily creamy, like crème brûlée. She imagines licking his inner thighs. Lifting the caramelized sugar— thin coating before digging with her tongue into his custard limbs. She pushes her parents' unethical idea in the back of her mind. They obviously do not understand her exceptional libido.

Elena is a shy and reticent person, and even more so as a student. When her teachers call on her, she imagines them being on top of her in a missionary position, and begins to hyperventilate. She gets distracted easily by educators. Educators who use language wisely and well. In fact, it would be so good for her libido if they recited the entire alphabet to her. Before they even got to the letter Q, her orgasm would subject her body to involuntary gestures. Her hand would automatically jerk up, as if to flap down the demonic flight of pleasure. The manner in which the educators curl their tongues, lick their lips, and the way the sound of one letter falls on another, on top of another letter, inner thighs, in a harmonic, oral-vibrating fashion, gets her clitoris into a disadvantaged frenzy.

Her teachers are aware of her social retardation. They are not aware, however, of her oral fixation, which is a fancy way of saying that she is sexually autistic. They go out of their way to accommodate her needs. Mrs. Wood, for instance, likes to pull her aside before her class begins to warn her of upcoming social traffic.

"Elena," Mrs. Wood softly speaks. "I'm calling on you today. Please try to breathe. Like this: Inhale, exhale." Mrs. Wood pinched her fingers together, and left them dangling above Elena's cheek as if she were a conductor swinging an invisible rod left and right.

On her way to her seat, she strips Mrs. Wood's sentences bare. Her mind fixates on Mrs. Woods' utterance of the words "on" and the word "you". She feels the vibration, the stacking of words: the "on" on top of the "you," and the train cars coming in between her legs. She is sensational. By the time she gets to her seat, her underwear is wet. Her clitoris, a piece of grapefruit, erupting. Her underwear, Pompeii. She grips her desk to remain steady.

At home she practices her speech in front of a glass. Inside, at the bottom of the glass, lies an ice cube. There, where no one is narcissistic or nude, she fixes her gaze.

"You're Abraham Lincoln and I'm going to talk about you to you! So, listen."

When Abraham Lincoln begins to melt and is slowly floating on himself, she clears her throat and begins.

"Abraham Lincoln, son of Thomas Lincoln and Nancy Hanks, was the sixteenth president of the United States. He was born on…on…on.." Elena trails off and begins to sob. She slumps down near the side of her bed and cries because her underwear is wet on the first letter "l" in Lincoln, and on "on."

Her mom notices her daughter's room, quiet like a nun.

"Elena, are you alright?" Her mother voices her concern, half-knocking on her door, half-gently plunging into her room. "Oh, what's wrong, sweetheart?"

Distraught, Elena shakes her head. Her mom slumps right down next to her, nudging her a little with her leg.

In between tears and sobs, Elena cries out, "Abraham Lincoln is a pervert!"

"Oh, honey!"

"All the presidents are perverts! Haven't you noticed how the letters in Lincoln's last name is similar to Clintons? It is the 'l's' and the 'o's' and the 'n's'! I just don't think it's fair!"

"What isn't fair, sweetheart?"

"The "l's" and the "o's". You know…?

She lets her mind drift. Her mother's voice shifts into the background and becomes white noise. Elena stares at her glass. She grips the neck of the neckless glass and pours the ice out. Water drips down the table. She cups the ice cube in one hand, and with the other hand she lifts the waistband of her underwear, and drops the ice cube down. She gasps quickly from the cold.

The ice cube having spent its brief life in the tunnel of the jeans short, spirals out of the short's helicoidal flight and lands on the wood floor.

Her mother pulls her socks off her feet and kneels on the floor. She begins to wipe the cold liquid from the floor and from the thighs of her child. She thinks her daughter is ready for a new president. Perhaps Roosevelt. Who lives in a wheel chair and can't possibly have white exotic thighs.

LOVE STORY WITH BIFURCATION AND VIOLATION

Thirty pounds of towels, socks, pants, pantyhose, underwear, bed sheets, hand towels, and one yellow handbag are pressed against the cement wall. You float into my mouth as we are leaning away from each other. And you ask the sky to bend. A cloudless expression shifts through the field. Your chest is falling through and tears bend over to the lake as you move out of my periphery. You float there once. With your mouth bouncing in between two spinning wheels. You float your face upward and I am bending to retrieve the pencil to scratch out your eyes. I'm weary of this picture. This silent gesture. You believe you can see better if I add more negative light, more shadow in between your eyelid and your cornea. I don't know what cornea means, if it stands for the dome or the eye itself, but cornea is coming closer to you. My heart keeps bending backward, exercising another muscle, rehearsing a different muscle, to get to you. My eyes are searching through the buses, mistaking the long chair for my sister and the handbag for my mother. Glimmers of light catch me in the middle of stretching out a caress. I fall easily for your earlobes. But you wouldn't take Eleanor. You wouldn't take her body with you on that war with a proper pronounciation. I had you at Eleanor. Your hand is touching me. You shift your pieces around and I remember where your underwear has not taken you. You are slipping slowly. And slowly the cornea returns to my body. My occupation. Your occupation. I haven't been able to scratch your eyes out. The pencil has a lead that isn't leading me. It's not marching to my eyesight. Is not marching toward my corridor. Your pencil is leading me across the room. To your face. I place your face in the palm of the page. You are not Virginia Woolf. I try to press Eleanor into you, but you call your mother instead. You call your mother when you are behaving. You leave me on the board. And you hoard the frame of a meaning. I am leaning now against the transpose of Tokyo. You are not there. I don't expect you there. After all, many Japanese women are kneeling. And you believe in height. You believe in retrieving containers from eye-level cabinets. You have a thing for breaking into the mouths of things and leaving them hanging open. The door hangs wide. And wider as I see the pools of light float on my face in black and white. Eleanor and uzi. Yes, you always do the uzi on me. This time it doesn't hurt. As you are winning and continue to win. You startle me once by slamming the brake on my throat. You are trying to stop the words from pumping out of my nostrils. There are millions of us ahead. Each second I release myself into the world. As I press into the wall and the luggage and the laundry is trying to shorten me. Your mouth is there by the window and if I walk closer to it, I can retrieve it. If I walk closer, I can open the wallet into your mouth. There is money there and a credit card I can swipe myself into a new blue skirt. The sun is receding as you are receding. I don't expect to cry in the bathroom alone. I don't expect for you to change your odor. I know now why the tears keep on falling away. I brush them away, not like a swipe with the credit card, but I am brushing them away like an airbrush, to make the color of my face even on the page of your body less watery. More color on paint. I will insert that page. No concert here. In the evening, the elbow of the pillow elbows my forehead, aiming for my eyes. I push my body away from the steamboat of that pillow, walking away from a dream. I ask you to hold my hands so that we can walk into a dream together when we sleep. But it's nothing like walking. A false step and we are diving. You ask me to stuff my body in Florida. You ask me to turn my skin inside out. You continue to check your email. You ask me not to check my email. You wish you were less wicked than the narrative hours. While your lungs continue to bleed, my legs are singing to my cornea. To your cornea. Scratching the program of the page. You had deceived me. You were not going to conceive me. You haven't been careful about the texture of your thought. I am not a fabric softener. You know this. I know this. We valued each other much less back then. Back then there was a swimming pool. You had it in you to keep me from drowning. You had it in you to put me in a good outfit. The summer above the balcony. The summer where your mouth is moving around the living room and the clashing is the table top. There are pages to be torn away. I gaze into the high chair we couldn't afford but which you got for me anyway.

Remember, you are not going to New York with me. But we arrive at Coney Island. We are alive, waking up the neighbors with the murmuring. The hotel. You haven't told the lilies about the hotel, the one in Houston, the one where I cut my toenails and you were painting the wall by panting. You took your boots into the bathroom. You took your boots there. You took my shoes in there as well, scrubbing the mud away. There were magnolias that were chasing after our shadows. We had been walking behind one another, making false accusations. We did not make it to Austin. We said hello to the greyhound. The black table your mother got for us. Had we forgotten to floss back then? Back then we had better cucumbers. Better floss. Better night gown. The headboard is so tall. Pregnant spiders think they can climb to heaven with it. And then there were plants that swung their legs back and forth, high in the ceiling and then my breath shortened and I could murmur the pork into being ochre or brown or red or like a sauce that we can suck our bones into. The sauce that expanded into the refrigerator walls like ivy or trellis or lungs. You remember now how you balanced your mouth in the teacup as the vapor refused to measure your chest. There are oranges and sangria and then lemons. I don't expect for you to sing back to me. There are repetitions and holes in the circumference of your falling. Your voice won't return to its complexity as you become fearless. You are holding the keys out to me and I was test driving your voice. When we first met, you allowed me to go into the dark with the wheels. There is structure and body contours and you were an ocean apart. You were parting my lungs. Convincing yourself that you can part my throat there. You float into the room, breaking each mouth into five consecutive parts. You had delivered the night before a plate of daffodils. In a black and white screen, the police officer asks his wife if she is okay. There are voices in the ocean calling one another. You ask me to become less and less. The melancholy is moving through the room. You have convinced yourself that people don't simply break the bones of a room. Remember that one time the police officer before a pile of books asked us to go to bed. Remember when you were holding her in your arms and I thought she is going to eat me? I am so fast to wake up. No coffee. No tea. No donut holes to spill my milk into. Lemongrass, bean spouts, green onion, and red onion were keeping us busy. You were busy receding. There were the night wars with the thermostat. There were other violent wars. Wars of the body, of art pages spilling out, of the toes, and then the way you kept moving your mouths. We will break even with our heartaches. You were not missing a key in your mind. You don't expect me to climb the windows. I used to come home to the texture of your nose pressing into the vellum of my mouth. You had a whole cashew hiding on the roof, slanting the light and then you had an intuitive field about throwing redolent fishes to neighbors. We had a battle of sound pollution to fight. We had those buses to climb into. We had the sea to ourselves. You carry your body into the room and you are lifting into the space jacket of the moment, vacuumed in by the melody of your arms and the way you softly lay the chestnut table on my chest. The way we are hiding each other in woods and you are opening your legs again to let a snowbank of salmon come crawling up to your body like sushi rolls. We are not asking ginger chicken to be duck skin. We are not asking for luxury. We are not asking for more donut holes. We are asking for breakfast by the vast window with sky that moves silently, invasive, out there in the cold. Do you remember Alabama or Big Sur? The desert you had spoken about. You were driving when the rocks were coming after you and I was bursting in and out of sleep. Do you remember then about the night that is persuasive? Do you remember where you were so unsure? Do

you remember the hippopotamus waiting for us at the McDonald driveway? Or was it Subway and we were trying to catch a
wink? The roof of the HHR. How we negotiate and renegotiate.
You were winning the lottery for us. And I was buying the
numbers with fingers. Buying into the hard corridor of time. Do
you remember the way you sung your lungs until it broke open?
You open the nights into the Houston sky. The rain that comes
through our chest. The way you were dancing ahead and I was
reading the geography of our desire. We have been fighting for
that depth. For those contours that were so uncertain of our
youth and our mouth. The resentment enters our seeds, spouting
out of our heartbeat. Do you remember the Houston sky? Do
you remember how it pours and how it rains. Or how heavy it
was. Do you remember? Do you remember how heavy the sky
was? We were two ants in a cremation jar. Was it plastic or was it
tin? Trying to run around in circles in that tin jar trying to avoid
the ashes, the cremation debris to stop falling on our head. But it
was raining in Houston. And Houston was crying into our
sleeves like a child. Do you remember the way the sleeves were
wet. And I had bought you flowers from the side of the street.
Near the bus. We are traveling through time together. Awake and
away from the lungs. We have been so careful not to be so far
away from our enemies. The men who are after the men. The
police who were after those bus riders who were getting on
without any tickets. You had wanted a free ride. Not a free
education. A free ride is important to people who had to decide
what had less protein, what is worse for them because it would
be cheaper. They wanted a free education for their legs. Caught
by the system. The police and then the Cy Tombly Music.
Everything is elevated at a certain height. You are not afraid
anymore. Of the body that hides in a dream. We were bathing in
the scratches. The childhood scratches. The way autumn doesn't

fall lightly into anyone's armpits. We were watching each other through the museums. And then the magnolias wouldn't stop gazing at us as if we were thunderstorms that were going to catch up to us. We have been wanting this night to open right away. There is more luggage to rearrange. The magnolias are fighting for their arrangement. You wouldn't know where to hide the key or chains or the odor after we had walked. We were walking out of the Japanese restaurant and we had made love in a modern museum. We were so near the Rothko painting and we want the odor inside us to reside. Those dark colors. Those field. There is solemnness and there is Joyce. How can we forget the afternoon? You were kissing me, taking me into your valves. Your volume going up and down. The bus tickets. After that we were climbing the stairs and you asked me to make love there. We had champagne and chicken and pepper and limes in the theater. We were always eating a full meal, a banquet. We made love under the seat. I was breathing then. You were breathing again and we had our bodies sprawled out. We lust over tomato juice. There was the Avocado thing and the soymilk. We had respective choices to make. We had things to carry across the living room. You were blowing your voice out, making managerial choices for a company. Your voice hurt and when you come home in the dark, to blow the day away. You read books and textures. And there is so much living room space you wanted to occupy. You had to occupy. I was searching for my mother in a chair and you were searching for your mother in an umbrella. I had been wanting so much for the proper tool of dancing. We were dancers. And then I noticed you were packing things away. Living another life before this life ends. You had the strainer. It's a beautiful one that allows the measuring cup not to fall through. The flours can't say too much about this. This perforation and this decoration. Your mother, your grandmother, and your family want to separate us

and my sisters and mother want to separate us, but you sold your
car and made payments to a credit card. I wish it was just for me.
You move away not carrying furniture with you. You had become
an avocado that I just wanted to peel under the Houston sun.
My eyes noticed the clouds and the persuasion and I could not
smell your bad odor. You are beautiful to me under any abrasion.
We loved each other and hovered over each other's voices. We
had love to conceive. We had bathroom to murmur. We had
those southern pools that dance our bodies into light and then
you were igniting the sea when we were tracing the footsteps.
Yes, we were behaving like thunderstorms. There is egg yolk and
the cucumber slices. I had missed bún riêu. There were tears
there. Wonderful breaths that dance in and out of each other's
chromosomes. You had cheesy air to break open. The credit
people were heading away. Leading the way. In my mother's
Lexus, we blew the sunflowers backward into your grave. We
brought half a dozen sunflowers and then we blew them back
into the earth in the desiccated graveyard of Nevada. We drive
through Sin City expecting an expedition of lust and find the
adventure in food coloring. We had the spread sheets. We had
toenails to cut. I was cutting my toenails in Houston. And in
Missouri, you pick me up from City Hall. Badges and scanners
and I didn't even understand the law of pepper spray as they
never trained me properly for it. We eat cake and we ate mon-
soons. We eat the bottom of a midnight dream and we expect to
know the different kinds of breakfast. The different kinds of
death. You return to the car door and we had walked Bella.
Remember the time you carried milk jugs on your back and I
was wrapping my hand around the head of a cilantro. Were you
waiting for your breath then? Were you waiting to ask for
another tomorrow? Yesterday, the field of dreams were delaying
their mountains and out came the thunderstorms that stab your

chest and the water was so light that they move sound around your armpits. There are laughers there that chase each other evenly unevenly. Uneventfully. Do you remember the drive back from Death Valley? We were scooping the earth into plastic bags and there were desert flowers in red and blue and that Mexican restaurant that you couldn't swallow down. The valleys and the desert and the dessert and the elevation. I could not satisfy you anymore. My heart rate had been increasing. You were waiting and then the silence came later. There was the driving. Waking up to Massachusetts. Waking up to Vermont. Waking up to Maine. You threw the journal into Maine. You threw it into the air, breaking the air open and the ripples that the marshy plants were trying to get to the pages. You were not singing to the body. You were not singing to the way the room maneuvers. You wanted to break me open into a thousand mirrors. Quiet. These things make my heart ache. The ride on the bus, your lips were red like the moon. The stars are falling, but your lips are red. Red in a dress. You were finding the corridors. Your lips were real diamonds. These things there are shopping sprees for. These things such as the salad spinner and the blender and the measurement cups we were aiming here. Remember when we didn't have a truck and we were wheeling the shopping cart. We were wheeling the shopping cart down the driveway. Pushing the mattress. Pushing our bodies forward. Do you remember you were cutting sadness out of the pages. Cutting sadness out of memory. You were cutting the edge and I was eating into the edge. I firmly believe in everything. Firmly believe in everything with your name in it. I believe you could conquer the world and that I am the bay that the wave recedes out. We said we would meet on the edge. My whole family gathered at the table and you resented not bringing your family. You had too many mouths to compete. You felt exposed. We were elated. I later discovered that you were eating a banana. I hadn't eaten at all. In a white dress that instead of blossoming out of my body sticks to my skin like children's stickers at a hospital. I think then of the virtue of being so sticky. The virtue of letting my exposure open their way. No one knows that you were eating a banana and that there is déjà vu. No one has to believe. No one has to see. I remember your white Volvo, looking like a bird, pecking on the highway. I remember driving in that bird while you caress my ears. My eyes on the road. And your eyes on my earlobes or my hair. You had the measuring cup in your mouth. Did you gaze down at the harsh wave? Did you when you were driving through wine country? While you snake in and out of fog? Did you remember the body of the earth, curvy thighs of the curvy ahead in the foggy road? Was it your lips and your eyes? Or something in you moving across too much distant and too much space? I want you and then I want you to make choices for us that are not there. Not available. Not kind to us. I remember now the eggrolls and tears were beaming off your eyelashes. I remember taking the bus from the airport. No, I hadn't been flying? I don't remember why we were there? You drove home without me. But love doesn't stick like butter. Not then. Do you remember the Christmas in Vegas? We purchased a Christmas tree that smelled like a Christmas tree. Do you remember how piney it was? How they delivered to us? And then we had one ball that we purchased from Goodwill. I remember telling my mother about the Christmas tree and being harassed over the phone. Nothing there is free and available. I had to stand in the quiet terrain for your inside. You don't believe I follow you from behind. You believe you had and you will continue to find me behind you. But my eyes are everywhere, searching for the appropriate cupcake for you. Searching for the eyeball in the brownie. The dark eyeballs that won't roll out of the socket of a serving plate. Do you remember walking on Houston's paved roads? Do you remember your boots thumbing the earth and we were singing margarita and carrot or maybe not. Do you remember on the Houston bed not staring at the Houston sky? There was dust everywhere. Our bodies are blown backward and forward by the dust and debris that curls under the body of the bus. We had an excuse to buy flowers. I had excuses to buy flowers. I buy flowers so that they oxidize the air we breathe. You take out your hands to receive and I put forth. Do you remember the Rothko? Walking along and find a pool that we couldn't dive in. I take each breath in. And then there were plates that you threw out of the window. And a bird in a form of a manuscript. In the darkness I collect your white birds with black texts and there its body tucked nearly underneath the trash receptacle. Do you remember wanting to push me in a shopping cart? Do you remember pushing your body forward? Me leaning like yogurt to one side because there were strawberries at the bottom that want to elevate to the cup's top? Do you remember the way I lean all the way to the side of the road. You were afraid that I had to die and that you were trying to get the other side, the more dangerous side, trying to protect my body from the coming traffic. Did you know that I didn't want you to die too? Do you remember the longing on the swivel chairs at Citi. You said the Citi people would expand. And who knew how to expand as much as anyone else. Parked in the car waiting for you to exit work with your lunch bag swinging left and right and your boots clicking. Left and right. Was it then that you stopped loving me or that things change? How wonderful were those tools that you use to excavate the heart that lies at the bottom of the marshland? I remember the bridge at Citi that you crossed. I recall the emblem of sorrow. There is night light from the ground that tips and radiates from the ground. When it casts onto your shirt, you are glowing like a pumpkin beneath that skin. Do you remember how to unlock it? And then you felt compelled to bring a luggage to carry the lunches we haul to work. At lunch we eat and I watch the smokers stand out in the cold losing their voices to winter. The gelid air and your car frozen in space. Your car won't move, and we are trying to exit one corridor to be in another corridor. My eyes are losing. We unfreeze each other from the mouth. We cling.

Acknowledgements

The author wishes to thank the following humans, friends, publishers, & editors: Tania Sarfraz, Andrew & Megan Wilt, Mike Corrao, Hanna Guido, Sam Moss, Jordan Castro, Gian DiTrapano, Claire Boyle, Patrick Cottrell, Sarah Gerard, Željka Marošević, Rachel James, Char McCutcheon, Tyler Mills, Amanda Fortini, Megan Milks, Michael Mejia, Raluca Albu, Steve Tomasula, Caitlin Forst, Denise R. Hansen, Twig and Barb Branch. And, at the Black Mountain Institute for their loving friendships and support: Sara Ortiz, Steve Siwinski, Niela Orr, Kellen Braddock, Michael Ursell, Lille Allen, Joshua Shenk, Miriam (&Laurie) Shearing, Sreshtha Sen, Wendy Wimmer, Summer Thomad, Layla Muhammad, and co-BMI fellows: Amy Kurzweil & Ahmed Naji.

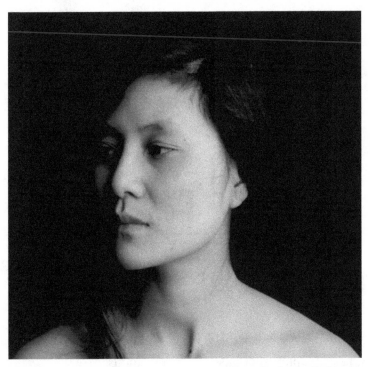

ABOUT THE AUTHOR

VI KHI NAO is the author of four poetry collections: *Human Tetris* (11:11 Press, 2019) *Sheep Machine* (Black Sun Lit, 2018), *Umbilical Hospital* (Press 1913, 2017), *The Old Philosopher* (winner of the Nightboat Prize for 2014), & of the short stories collection, *A Brief Alphabet of Torture* (winner of the 2016 FC2's Ronald Sukenick Innovative Fiction Prize), the novel, *Fish in Exile* (Coffee House Press, 2016). Her work includes poetry, fiction, film & cross-genre collaboration. She was the Fall 2019 fellow at the Black Mountain Institute: https://www.vikhinao.com

11:11 Press is an American independent literary
publisher based in Minneapolis, MN.
Founded in 2018, 11:11 publishes innovative
literature of all forms and varieties. We believe
in the freedom of artistic expression, the
realization of creative potential, and the
transcendental power of stories.